© 2015 Copyright By Michael Paterson

Our Destiny

Ch

On my way to Monday classes, I ... girlfriends' apartment to pick up ... ...ert there yesterday. I got to the 4th floor an... ...ed the door, using the key that she had given me months ago. I really didn't expect anyone to be there, she should have been at school, so I was surprised to hear some moans coming from the bedroom down the hall. Had I not had to go into the second bedroom that served as an office/computer room, I probably would never have heard the moaning.

My curiosity was aroused, I walked silently down to the bedroom door that was open just a few inches. There on the bed was my beloved Lynsy with one of the football players pounding into her. The moans I heard were Lynsy approaching orgasm. Her head was thrown back on the bed, eyes rolled to the back of her head as she called out for Todd, the football player, to give her more and more.

I was in total shock but I did grab my cell and take a few photos and a short video of her calling out that she had never had it so good and that he (Todd) was getting better every time. My heart sank to the floor to find that not only was the love of my life cheating, she'd probably been doing it for quite a while. How long, I didn't know, or at this point, care.

I turned away from the bedroom, tears blurring my eyes and heart breaking in my chest. Instead of leaving right away, I took the time to quickly and quietly as possible pack up my laptop and all the various disks and items of mine that were in the computer room. I just tossed them into the bag, not worrying about neatness or order as I usually would. I had no plans of ever coming back here again. There were some clothes in the bedroom closet as well. Obviously, there was no way to get them.

I didn't care anymore at that point. As I walked out, I took a quick look around and spied a photo of me and Lynsy in better times sitting on the coffee table. There were some highlighters and markers on the dining table that served as her desk. I took the black one and with a heavy heart, in large, bold strokes, put an X across the photo, then placed it on the table next to the books that Lynsy was supposedly studying. She wouldn't be able to miss it, or the message.

I left the apartment as silently as I had come in, throwing my key on the floor just inside the door. I wouldn't need it again. I don't think they even heard me leave or knew that I had been there. A little about Lynsy and me. My name is Mike Foster. I'm not what you'd call good looking or a jock or anything. I've got brown straight hair that I wear fairly short and grey eyes. I'm not overly muscular or anything, but not a bunch of flab either. I think average would be a good description.

I grew up in a small town in the heart of British Columbia. Lynsy Brown and her family had moved into our neighbourhood when Lynsy was three. I was a year older. Her parents and mine became close friends over the years and Lynsy and I basically grew up together. She was my best friend, and we shared everything throughout the years, from the first date to the first kiss (on the swing behind her house) to almost the first everything. Through junior high school and then high school we were pretty much inseparable. We became known as LM since she was Lynsy and I was Mike.

We gave our cherries to each other the night of my graduation prom. It wasn't the normal quickie in the backseat of a car at lover's lane, but a night of unbridled sex and passion in a hotel suite near downtown. While our parents weren't thrilled with it, they accepted the inevitable. My dad even remarked that he was surprised that we had waited that long. Though we had done some heavy petting and oral through high school we had made a pact that we would hold off on "doing it" until I graduated. It was magnificent, and I pictured the two of us together forever.

Even when I went away to college, we kept in touch and she would come to visit me or I'd come home on weekends. During the year that I was in college and she was finishing high school, I don't think we spent any more than ten weekend days apart except during exams. Then it was a little longer but not much.

When Lynsy graduated, she got a full scholarship to the same college I was attending. Her major was biology with a view to the future in the medical field. I was working my way through as a tech support guy for the college computer network. As well as getting a fairly good pay cheque, the experience was invaluable since it mirrored real-world conditions that I would eventually move on to.

Already I had had some head-hunters showing an interest in me because of my grades, and the work I did on the college computer network. I also did some one-on-one tutoring for some of the students who needed help in math or some other courses related to the computer systems program. When Lynsy started at the college, she didn't want any part of the dorm life, and the thought of sororities and that lifestyle left her cold, so she coerced her father into renting an apartment not too far from the college. I, on the other hand, lived in the dorms because it was affordable, and I was paying my own way.

My parents couldn't afford to pay my way through college, but the job with a good paycheque, as well as the money I made tutoring, made my life fairly comfortable for a student. I hardly ever saw my roommate, but we seemed to get along just fine. Neither one of us were partiers, and my roommate, was one of the quietest and cleanest college guys you'd ever find. Granted, our room could usually be cluttered and messy, but we weren't really slobs.

Anyway, with Lynsy living not too far away and having her own apartment, it was like we had died and gone to heaven. We quickly fell into a routine that had us together one or two nights a week and inseparable on weekends. I'd come over to the apartment on Friday afternoon after finishing class. By the time Lynsy got home, I'd have dinner started (yup, I can cook) and a bottle of wine chilling in the fridge. Life was good, and I thought we would eventually move on to the next logical step of becoming man and wife once we had finished our schooling.

Well, that was then and this is now.

After leaving the apartment for my last time I trudged back to the college, my gut feeling like I was going to be sick any second and my heart just absolutely crying. I didn't even bother going to class. There was no way I'd get anything out of the lectures in my present mindset. I dropped off my stuff in my dorm and made my way over to the cafeteria that was sort of a central meeting place for all the students.

I didn't want company, so I grabbed a large coffee, black no sugar, and found a table way in a secluded corner where I could just sit by myself and ponder the events of the morning. I had just sat down when my cell buzzed. Lynsy. I didn't answer just let it go to voicemail. Then I programmed the phone to block any more calls from her cell, the landline at the apartment, and even her number back at home. Let her call, it would go nowhere now.

I don't know how long I'd been sitting there; long enough for my coffee to get cold. I'd hardly touched it. I gradually became aware of a person sitting across and down at the other end of the table. It was Leah Brown, a classmate. She was one of those people you would never notice in a crowd. Very quiet and introverted. I don't think we'd spoken more than half a dozen times in the two plus years we'd been in the same program.

She was known as one of the brains of the class but I'd never had any real interaction with her. I had never seen her at any of the functions, and couldn't even recall seeing her dating anyone. She was the type of person that seemed to be taken for granted. There, but not really there. As I said, she is the type you wouldn't really notice. The few times we had spoken, I recalled being quite comfortable talking to her.

Anyway, I became aware that she was talking. "Mike, you okay? You weren't at the lectures this morning. Not that you missed much. Old man Adams went off on one of his tangents and wasted a whole period. You look like a big thundercloud is hanging over your head. You okay?"

I waited for a second or two, trying to figure out what to say to her without losing it. "Hi Leah, yeah it's not a good day." I didn't elaborate further.

"You need someone to talk to? I'm a great listener."

"I don't ... I'm not sure that...God Leah," I began to do exactly what I'd feared and could feel the tears welling in my eyes. "It's just that I...I...oh goddammit, I caught Lynsy with one of the football players - Todd the linebacker."

"What do you mean you caught..." the question died on her lips as she realized what I was saying, "Oh my God Mike, I'm so, so sorry. You two seemed to be destined..."

"I guess "seemed" is a pretty good description. I don't think I ever want to see her again. And as for Todd...well let's just say I hope they're happy together." My voice must have been rising since I could see some others at nearby tables looking over my way. I got up from the table and made my way out of the cafeteria and began walking back to my dorm. Actually, I didn't want to go there either.

Almost numb, I stood just inside an emergency exit and the tears began in earnest. I don't know how long I stood there, tears pouring down my face. I noticed that Leah had joined me, just standing beside me quietly, not saying anything. Just watching.

"Go away, Leah. I'm lousy company. You don't need any of this." I angrily wiped the tears from my face. "Just leave me. Go."

She didn't move, instead placed her small hand on my arm. "Mike, you're hurting right now. You need someone to talk to, to listen. It'll help you through the pain, and you must be in so much pain. I don't think I can even really understand it. But I'm a good listener."

I started walking, going nowhere in particular. I sensed, more than saw that Leah was walking with me. Almost unconsciously I began to relate how we had grown up together, became lovers when I graduated from high school, and how our love had grown over the past year in college. Then I told her about what had happened this morning. We'd walked a good long way, and found ourselves in a neighbourhood quite away from the college.

"Mike, I have to ask. Did you actually see them...?"

I abruptly cut her off and angrily said, "See them. Yeah, I saw them. Fucking like two rabbits in heat!" I pulled my phone out of my pocket and brought up the photos I had taken that morning showing the date and time, then to ice the cake, I showed Leah the video where Lynsy was crying out how good Todd was, and she'd never had it so good. Leah watched the video and her eyes got bigger and bigger, and her face quickly became bright red.

"My God, I've never seen anything like that. I've heard of it, but didn't think I'd ever see it, let alone with people I knew." She was almost stuttering the words because of the effect the video had on her. "My God, my God," she kept whispering.

"Seen enough? I have. I haven't decided what I'm going to do with this, but it will be something. As the saying goes, don't get mad, get even, and I WILL get even." I almost spat the words out. "I will get even. Oh my God, Lynsy. Why? Why? Why?" I began to lose it again and collapsed onto a nearby transit bench.

To give her credit, Leah didn't try to stop the tears this time either. She just sat there and watched my world implode. After a while, she quietly said, "Mike, let's get back or we're gonna get soaked. Rain's coming and it's supposed to be a hell of a storm."

"You go ahead. Just leave me. You don't need any of this grief, and it has nothing to do with you."

"You're right. It has nothing to do with me. But I see a friend, well a classmate anyway, who's hurting. Hurting terribly. I don't really know the hurt you're going through, but I know it's bad. Don't you think for a second that this is some kind of burden you're laying on me? You're hurting and I want to help."

"Yeah, whatever. Leah, I appreciate what you're saying. I do, really. But right now I think it's best that I am alone. Just me and that huge cloud over my head. Please, just go. I'll be okay."

"Okay, Mike. I'm going. But if you need a sympathetic ear here's my cell. You're the only one I've given it to so I'd appreciate it if you don't give it out."

"Thanks, Leah. If I need a shoulder, you'll be the first."

"I hope so." With that, she gathered her things together and began the long walk back to campus. I just sat on the bench, staring at the ground. There must have been half a dozen busses go by, each one stopping for this dejected looking man, and each, in turn, being waved on.

After a while I stirred and began walking back to campus, the rain had started. It got heavier and heavier but he hardly noticed. By the time I got back to the dorms, I was absolutely drenched and chilled to the bone. Shivering, I stripped off my wet clothes and went into the shower. The hot water chased away the chill, and I tried to formulate a plan. It didn't work. I was just too numb, too hurt. I got out of the shower, pulled on some sweats and collapsed onto my bunk. I pulled the covers up over my head, and quickly, mercifully went to sleep.

Sometime later, the strident ringing of the phone on his desk woke me. Let it ring. There was no one I wanted to talk to. It went to the answering machine.

"Mike, Mike. It's me, Lynsy. Pick up. Please oh please pick up. Please, let me explain. It's not..."

I got up from the bed and pulled the phone plug out of the wall. Explain? What to explain? She cheated on me. By her own words, it wasn't the first time, just the first time they got caught.

I went back to bed. This time sleep eluded me.

Chapter 2

Next morning my mood matched exactly the dark, threatening sky. I decided that I should at least try to attend lectures today. Maybe they'll take my mind off of the hurt, for at least a little while. I wasn't really hungry, but stopped off at the cafeteria and grabbed a large coffee, then made my way to the computer lab. Rules said that there wasn't supposed to be any food or drink in the lab, but today I didn't care about the rules.

I went to a computer at the back of the room instead of my usual place closer to the front. Today was just a lecture so seating didn't matter. Hardly anyone noticed that I was there. I looked around and noticed that Leah wasn't there yet. Not like her to be late for, let alone miss, a class. The lecture began and I was able, for a short while, put all the events of yesterday on the back shelf. Later, I found myself wondering what English was going to be like since Lynsy and I shared that class. I remembered that quite a few players from the football team were in that class too, along with us "nerds" from the computer science program. Oh well, I'd have to cross that bridge when I got to it, but I sure wasn't looking forward to the ordeal.

Ultimately the lecture ended, and I was off to English. I had really considered skipping this class, and just getting the notes from one of the other students, but then I thought to myself that neither Lynsy nor Todd were going to cause me to miss any more classes if I could help it. The best thing I could do was show up, and just totally ignore them. The best revenge, for now, was to graduate with a 4.0. I'd get to them later, I don't know how or when, but my time will come.

And that's pretty much what happened, except neither Lynsy nor Todd had shown up for English class, though Leah did make an appearance. She gave me a slight, friendly wave and then took her normal seat down near the front of the lecture room. Unusually, I was further back. When I had been with Lynsy, we sat closer to the front, sort of in the middle of our friends and acquaintances. Not today, and probably not ever again.

Classes over for the day, I headed back to my dorm and tried to get my life and my mind back on track. Ed had come and gone, leaving a note that there were a bunch of messages from Lynsy and maybe I should phone her and find out what's going on. Not a chance of that. I went over to the phone and hit the erase button twice, deleting all the voice messages. I remembered that I had unplugged it yesterday; Ed must have plugged it back in while he was here.

I got into some track gear planning a long run where I didn't have to think about anything, just listen to the tunes on my Walkman. I was going down the stairs and had almost got to the entrance when Todd came in. He glanced at me then looked away. I ignored him, exited the building and started my run. There's no way he'd know that I knew that he and Lynsy had been doing the horizontal hula unless he was still there when she saw my not-too-subtle message. Whatever. Too fucking bad for him.

The run felt good. I could feel the tension of the last day gradually easing and I loped down the bike/running paths that wound throughout the neighbourhood. I gradually became aware of someone coming up behind me. I glanced over my shoulder and almost stumbled. Fuck, I thought, Lynsy. Just who I didn't want or need. I darted across the street, dodging oncoming traffic. Thankfully, I saw that she couldn't follow me right away, and I managed to put a lot of distance between us. I varied my route, but did continue my run and didn't see Lynsy again.

For the next few weeks, life went on and I was slowly, ever so slowly, getting used to being on my own. I'd been able to change my English class, so I wouldn't have any reason to run into Lynsy. Ed told me, through his girlfriend who knew Lynsy, that after the first week or so, Lynsy had stopped looking for me or trying to contact me. He had also told her, when she showed up at the dorms, that he didn't know where I was.

I appreciated that and told him so. I didn't go out of my way to avoid her but don't recall ever seeing her during the next months. Leah was encouraging, letting me know that there was a friendly shoulder to cry on or someone who cares that would listen. I thanked her but didn't call. The hurt and the betrayal were far too fresh in my mind. It would be a long while before I would trust someone again.

Friends we had socialized with knew that something had happened. When pressed, I would tell them to go ask

Lynsy. Gradually they drifted out of my life. Oh, we were cordial and would chat, but the social life we once enjoyed together just wasn't there. I became somewhat of a hermit, just classes, work and tutoring. The word got out; don't try to discuss Lynsy with me. It was a taboo subject and that was not open to negotiation.

It was nearing Christmas break when my mother phoned to ask if I was going to make it home for the holidays. I felt a pang of guilt for not being in touch with her more often, either phoning or email. Truth be told, I hadn't really thought much about it. "Mom, I'm not too sure I'd be good company. Something's happened and it's not going too well right now."

"Listen, Mike, your sisters and brother expect their big brother to be home for Christmas. You know how they love to hear you talk about all the stuff going on at the university and the work you've done. I know you can't really afford any gifts, but that's alright. We just want our oldest son and big brother home for Christmas."

"But, Mom..."

"No buts. If it's bus fare you need or gas money or something, we can help."

"No, it's not that Mom. I can afford whatever I need. You know I've got a good job here at the university, and I tutor some of the other students as well. No, It's something worse that I have to work out for myself."

"You're not in any trouble...?"

"No, Mom. Maybe you should phone Lynsy's mom and find out. It really hurts too much to talk about it, even after a couple of months."

"What are you talking about? Are you having problems with Lynsy? That, I can't believe. You two are like peas in the proverbial pod."

"Were, Mom, were. We WERE like two peas in the pod."

Dead silence on the other end, then quietly, "Oh Mike, I'm sorry. I didn't know. You must be hurting so bad..."

"Yeah Mom, I think part of me has died. I wouldn't be much fun to be around, so I think I'll just stay here and work. There's a Christmas dinner held here for kids who can't get home, so it won't be just me."

We chatted about nothing in particular for a few more minutes, then ended with a promise that I would at least think about coming home, even for a few days. I was so miserable, so hurt, felt so betrayed that the thought of going home and being "normal" made me break out in a cold sweat.

I'd been mentally kicking around an idea for a few weeks; now I made a decision to act on it. I knew exactly what I will do. My mind played out various scenarios over the next few days as my plan formed. The hurt would go away, permanently.

I didn't know it at the time but I had fallen into a deep depression. I knew something was wrong, very wrong. The problem was, I didn't know how to get help, and felt that I had no one to ask. All the extra work I'd been doing, the hard work doing assignments, even the extra tutoring had only dulled the pain, pushing it into a corner of my mind for short periods of time. Gradually I sank into the black hole, seeing no way out.

One of the dorm-rats had acquired an over-under 12 gauge shotgun. There were really strict rules about firearms in the dorms, but somehow this guy had not only managed to smuggle it in but kept it in the back of his closet. His dorm room was right below mine and laid out exactly the same. I knew I would have no problem breaking into the room. The locks were a joke. During our first orientation, the standing joke was that if you didn't want anything stolen, leave your door open. A locked door was an invitation to a break in.

Anyway, I knew I could get my hands on it if it was still there. First I had to say some goodbyes and write my final letter. The letter would be hard. My family would be crushed for a while, and even some of my friends would be hurt. They would gradually get over their hurt. Mine would be ended forever, and that thought kept me functioning.

Writing the letter was harder than I thought. The first few drafts were just the ramblings of a lost person. They really made no sense, though at the time they were written they seemed like masterpieces. Many hours, and many revisions later, I had finished it. What I had written would have to do. Now the rest of the plan was set in motion. It was just over a week until Christmas. Almost everyone who was leaving for the break had gone leaving the few of us that hadn't planned on going home hanging around.

To my surprise, I found that my roommate was staying since his girlfriend lived here in town. He'd be spending most of the holidays with her and her family. He assured me that he'd check in every once in a while to make sure I wasn't getting into trouble. Fat chance of that; of course I didn't tell him of my plans. Another surprise was that Todd was staying as well. I found out that his grades weren't too good (I had flatly told him to find another tutor, but never told him why). He wasn't able to find someone so here he was cramming during the festive season. Too bad, so sad.

The next day was totally winter. The wind howled through the trees and the buildings. No-one stayed outside any longer than absolutely necessary. Snow was blowing almost horizontally, drifting into deep piles against any vertical surface it could find. A totally miserable day that mirrored my totally miserable feelings. The dorms were deserted. Everyone had hurried off to where ever they were going. I wouldn't be interrupted.

I went down one floor and easily broke into the dorm room where I knew the gun had been kept. A cursory search may not have found it, but I did. And I even found some ammunition for it. I'd only need one but decided to load both barrels.

I took my time and went back to my room. The Christmas carols playing on the stereo did nothing to lighten my mood. In fact, I think they made it worse. They sounded plastic and phoney. Peace on Earth? Give me a fucking break. Tell that to the men and women in Afghanistan or Iraq. Even my favourite R&B station had gotten into it. I turned the stereo off and lay down on my bed. I must have dozed off. It was afternoon when I awoke. The storm outside showed signs of abating. Whatever. I wouldn't be caring about the weather for much longer.

I got the letter I had written and opened it up to re-read, just to make sure I'd said everything I wanted, in the way I wanted.

My letter:

Dear friends and family.

By now, since you're reading this, you'll know that I am dead by my own hand. I know that some of you will be terribly hurt by this, and wonder if there was something you could have done to prevent it. Please, don't waste your time on self-blame. It won't bring me back, a fact which I am thankful for, and will solve nothing. Grieve if you must, but get on with your lives.

To my family. This is the hard part. Will you ever understand what drove me to this point? What caused me, a relatively normal human being, to take such a drastic step? Could you have done anything? I really can't give you an answer to that, but I can explain why.

When I caught Lynsy with Todd, my whole world ended. I have tried, tried so hard over the past couple of months to come to terms with what happened and move on. Unfortunately, my sense of loss, sense of hurt, sense of betrayal got worse with time, not better.

I have not talked to Lynsy since that terrible day. There's nothing she could have said that would have taken away the pain, and no explanation would have eased the hurt and betrayal. Yet, even though she wounded me so terribly, I still love her. I absolutely loathe what she did, and don't know why she did it. I am afraid that if I confronted her, I would lose it and hurt her the way she hurt me, and I can't do that.

Will she feel guilty? Maybe, but at this point, I don't much care. I hope she and Todd are happy; they deserve each other.

To my brother and sisters. I know this will hurt you, just as it will Mom and Dad. I only wish that I had been a better big brother. You deserve much better than I could give, especially these last few months. Just remember the few good times we had together. Grow up and be the responsible citizens I know you can be. Remember, I do love you, and will be watching over you.

To my parents. I know and understand that this will shock and hurt you terribly. Nothing I can write will alleviate that. You have supported me and helped me more than you know, and more than I ever gave you credit for, and for that I'll be eternally grateful.

But right now, I can't see my way out of all of this. All I can see is this total darkness all around me and no way out of it. In fact, it gets worse each day, and I can't live with that anymore. At this point, all I want is the pain to go away. No one, least of all you, need to be burdened with my problems. I feel that this way is better for all of us, and you shouldn't have this dark cloud hanging over your head. Yes, you will hurt. Hurt badly. But please look at it from my point of view. I feel that I have nothing left to live for. I do love you. I think this way is best for all of us.

I signed the bottom, folded it carefully and placed it in the envelope on the table, addressed to "The Person Who Finds Me"

It was time. I lay down on my bed again, took the shotgun and placed the barrel under my chin. With some difficulty, I managed to get my thumbs on both triggers. It was time to go...

Chapter 3

The door opened and Ed stuck his head in. His cheerful call of "Merry Christmas" died as he saw me on my bed. He ran over to the bed and after a brief struggle wrestled the gun away from me before I could pull the triggers. "Dude, what the fuck's with that? You fuckin' crazy, man?" he ranted on for a few seconds, not really giving me a chance to answer. I realized then that I had failed and buried my head in my pillow and totally lost it. Ed called 911 and explained the situation, letting them know that there was still a loaded gun in the room. Help was on the way.

I heard a commotion at the door and looked up to see a few of the students who were staying behind for the holidays crowding the door. One of them was Todd. They were all shouting together trying to get from either Ed or me what was going on. At that point, I don't really know what came over me, but I managed to reach for the still loaded gun. I yelled at Todd, "You son of a bitch! You asshole! You caused it, you and that whore!"

The others scattered as he stood in the door with a totally shocked look on his face when I pointed the gun toward him. "Jesus, no! Don't, don't..." I pulled both triggers and saw him stagger backwards and slump to the floor of the hallway. Time seemed to stop. In a sort of fog, I carefully opened the gun, ejected the spent shells then placed it on the bed. The police would see that it was no threat to them. Ed stood in shock, his face white as a ghost, ears ringing from the twin blasts of the gun. He just stood there, looking first at Todd lying in the hallway, and then at me, almost as if he couldn't comprehend what had just happened.

Sirens got louder, then stopped and we heard loud footsteps as the first responders ran up the stairs. I saw one officer, weapon drawn bend down to check on Todd. His partner cautiously looked into the room, saw no immediate threat and ordered Ed and me face down on the floor. The two of us secure, he quickly checked the shotgun, then advised his partner that the place was secure.

After a few minutes, with discussion from several of the students who had seen what was going on, Ed was released. I was advised of my rights and placed under arrest. The officer escorted me down to the police car and placed me in the back, still handcuffed. I didn't know if Todd was dead or alive, as a matter of fact, my brain had just sort of shut down. It was sort of like I was watching a scene from a movie. So far, except to acknowledge my rights, I hadn't spoken a word. That's pretty much the way it would be until my trial except when I talked to my lawyer.

The police advised me that Todd was badly injured, and probably wouldn't survive. I don't remember if I ever acknowledged that statement. I was taken to the cells, processed, and fingerprinted. They took away everything I had except my socks and boxers and gave me a set of coveralls to wear. I just did as they said without replying or saying anything, and I ultimately found myself in a cell, alone.

They had asked me if I wanted to say anything. I shook my head "no". Then they asked if I wanted a lawyer. I just shrugged my shoulders. At this time, they would have saved everyone a lot of trouble and expense if they just shot me and had done with it but that wasn't their job. I found out later that they had phoned my parents who arranged for the duty lawyer to act for me, and the slow wheels of the legal system began to turn. I learned the next day that Todd had died from his wounds. For some reason, I felt nothing, no shame, no elation. I was still numb.

Against my lawyers' advice, I intended to plead guilty during my first appearance. We had discussed my case at some length after our first meeting, and he felt that I had a case for diminished capacity. I told him in no uncertain terms that I didn't want a long drawn out trial, and that yes, I had killed a man, and there was no diminished capacity.

Without going into all the details, it ended up that the letter I had written, as well as statements from several witnesses, indicated that I had intended to end my own life, and had no intention of killing Todd. I ended up getting seven years for manslaughter, with the first year to be served in a mental institution because of my depressed state.

Throughout the ordeal, my parents had been behind me. Upon sentencing, my mother broke down, as mothers would. My dad stoically sat beside her, a look of deep sadness on his face. I had only spoken to them a couple of times. Most of what they knew came from the trial, and their lengthy discussions with Mr Purdy, my lawyer. I also noticed that Lynsy's mother was sitting next to Mom. She looked as hurt as I felt.

I was led away, and my new life began. The mental institution was an eye opener, but also a blessing in disguise. Up to that time, depression had been just a vague concept attributed to weak people who couldn't or wouldn't help themselves. Over the next year, I found out more, a lot more. Looking back, I was I classic case and if I had recognized the symptoms, there was lots of help available. I hadn't known.

After the year in a hospital, I was transferred to prison. In the mental hospital, because of my circumstances, I was closely monitored and had little freedom of movement. Everywhere I went, I had an escort, though most of the time I wasn't handcuffed or shackled. They came to realize that I was no threat and that I would do exactly what I was told. I still had my escort everywhere, and when I was transferred to a prison he actually shook my hand and gave me a brief hug, and wished me good luck.

My cellmate turned out to be a huge black guy. I was 5"10" and maybe 180 pounds soaking wet. Sam was at least 6'4" and probably outweighed me by a hundred pounds. Maybe the stories I'd heard about being "Bubba's lady" were true. Although my depression was at least sort of controlled, I still didn't much care whether I lived or not, so the cell arrangements didn't really matter to me.

Sam, my cellmate, had earned the privilege of a computer, something I wouldn't do for at least 6 months.

Other than nodding his head when the guards brought me to the cell, he had totally ignored me. I watched as he struggled to work the machine. I didn't know, at the time, what he was trying to do, but I could see it wasn't going well.

"What are you doin' man?"

"What's it to you, white boy?"

"Just thought I might be able to help."

"Yeah, right. What do you think I am, just some dumb fuckin' nigger that can't operate a simple computer?"

"Nope, what I see is a guy who has never been taught how to use it. There's a whole lotta difference. If you want to learn, I can teach. I was a computer science major in college. I may not know shit about being a prisoner, but I know about computers."

"Yeah, well, we'll see." And with that, a friendship was born. Over the next few months, using his computer because I hadn't yet earned the privilege, I taught him the ins and outs of the hardware, what each component did and how they ultimately all worked together to end up doing whatever on the screen. I found Sam to be an insightful student, absorbing the knowledge like a sponge.

The only thing he couldn't get a hold on was programming. I explained to him that you sort of had to be wired that way. Not all was lost because there's lots more to computers than programming. If he had a good solid knowledge of the hardware, and a background in networking he could get work almost anywhere.

We bonded over the next few years. At the start, some of the members of various gangs had marked me for whatever purpose. Sam had let it be known in no uncertain terms that they would have to deal with him if anything happened to me. I wasn't his "lady", I was his teacher, and to them I was inviolate. My job to start with had been in the laundry, the worst of the worst as far as jobs available in prison. I came to see just how bad some of the men in here were, though I was pretty much left alone. The threat of having to deal with Sam saw to that.

After about two years I was called into the wardens' office. Word had gotten out that I was able to teach about computers. He wanted to know if I could teach computer classes to interested inmates who had earned the privilege. He had my file open on his desk so I knew that he was aware of my background. Apparently, some of the guards had seen what I was doing with Sam, and the word had gotten back to the warden. The powers that be were impressed that I seemed to know my stuff and wanted to get a trial program up and running.

The warden and I discussed this at some length, and finally, he told me to get a list of things I would need to teach a class of 10 students. It would be an experiment at first, to see how well it was received, and also how well I could teach. I got the list together, gave it to one of the guards, and pretty much let the whole thing slip from my mind. I was happy to just be teaching Sam, and I had "graduated" from the laundry to doing work outside in the yard, picking up litter, sweeping, and menial jobs. I loved it; well, as much as I could under the circumstances.

During this time, Sam introduced me to weight-lifting. He told me that he had always lifted, and kept it up in prison while he could. He showed the correct ways and coached me as I slowly began to develop a toned physique. I was no longer the out of shape geek, but a toned and in shape geek. I had also learned that Sam would be getting out of prison around the same time as me if neither of us was granted an early parole. I applied of course but was turned down. I hadn't really expected any other outcome. I never did apply for it again.

About six months after my talk with the warden, I was again called into his office. I wasn't sure what trouble I was in because you don't, get called to his office for nothing. I had totally forgotten about the proposed computer program.

The prison would get a fully equipped computer lab with an instructors' station and stations for ten students. At first, the program would concentrate on basic repair and maintenance, and operating system support. Gradually it would evolve into networking. There would be no internet access from the lab. I was to develop a curriculum for approval, and they hoped to have the whole thing up and running in about a month or so.

"Mike," the warden told me just as I was leaving his office, "this is a real opportunity for you and the other inmates. You've done well here so far, and we're pleased with your progress. Don't blow it."

"Warden, I totally fucked up my life once. I don't plan on letting that happen again. You won't be sorry for this, sir." I floated back to my cell to give Sam the good news, then set to work developing a course for a bunch of people I didn't know, about a subject they probably know little if anything about. If I had been on the outside, it would have been heaven. As it was, it was probably as good as it could be.

Finally, the big day came. The computers had been delivered, along with all the teaching material I had requested. I spent a week setting up the lab and had tried to get Sam assigned as my assistant. They would wait and see. Only the best behaved that showed an interest would be allowed to attend. Classes would be an hour in the morning and again one hour in the afternoon. Homework could be assigned at my discretion. At best, it could only be reading. After hours, the lab was locked down and no one had access to it.

After I had transferred to prison, I began to study and work towards my degree through the universities' distance learning program. When I had left, I only had about a year and a half to go to graduate. Here, I had at least six years in which to do that, and I still had over three years to go when the experimental program began. As far as prison went, this was as good as it could get.

I was back on track for my degree, and I had something positive to contribute. I learned that with good behaviour, more privileges were granted, and if they weren't abused, and if you didn't get "written up" for breaking the rules, life behind bars would at least be tolerable. Of course, I had killed a man and would have to do my time, but it didn't need to be hard time.

During my incarceration, my parents came every month for a visit. My mom, for some reason, looked a little better each time, but I could see that Dad's health was failing. The only ground rules I had with them were there was to be no discussion whatever about Lynsy and what had happened. All that was over, and eventually I would get out and begin a new life. My brother and sisters always sent their love and sent small presents of items that were treasured such as toothpaste, toothbrushes, and other toiletries which I willingly shared with Sam and a few others who had become sort of friends.

About four years into my sentence I was called to the wardens' office. I knew it wasn't about the computer classes, they were going well and the guards had been giving good reports on the program. No, this time it was a family thing. My father had died of a massive heart attack. Because of my good behaviour, I was to be given a two-day parole to attend his funeral. I would be accompanied by a guard, and we would be leaving the next morning.

The warden expressed his condolences and said that he hoped this wouldn't have any detrimental effect on the computer classes. I assured him that it wouldn't if I could help it since my Dad would be up there watching over me and I knew he'd kick my ass if I screwed up.

The guard and I attended the funeral. He wasn't too bad and gave me some extra time to spend with my family. Because I wasn't considered a flight risk, there were no shackles or handcuffs. I had given my word, and that seemed to be enough. My Mom explained that Dad had been slowly going downhill since I was sent to prison, whereas she seemed to flourish. She said it was because she had someone to care for that really needed her help and that worrying about me and my situation wouldn't be any good to anyone.

I felt that maybe she had missed her calling and should have become a nurse. The funeral, of course, was a sad event. I wasn't allowed any contact with anyone other than the minister and my immediate family. I didn't realize how many friends my parents had until I saw the crowd at the cemetery. I knew people had wanted to talk to me, to give me their regards and condolences, but I was kept away from everyone by the guard.

As the graveside service commenced I looked around at the people and realized that I knew most of them from when I had been growing up here in town. I wondered if I would ever see any of them again, for I knew at that moment that I probably wouldn't be coming back here again. I thought I saw Lynsy in the back of the crowd, but couldn't be sure. Her parents were here since they had been good friends of the family for almost my entire life.

It was almost with relief that I returned to the prison. True to my word, I hadn't even thought about running for it. The guard, of course, had to report on my behaviour. I guess it was a good report. The computer classes evolved. There wasn't much turnover in students, and those that came were, at least to all appearance, willing to learn. I had started with the very basics, similar to the way I had learned, graduating from installing hardware, memory, and other components, to troubleshooting the hardware.

In the end, most could diagnose hardware problems and provide the solution with little help from me. Teaching the operating system support was more difficult. We took it in baby steps, how Windows did what it did, its role in the operation of the computer, why it did what it did, and the major causes of the myriad of problems it could have. I had barely touched the basics, but it would have to do. Anything further in depth was way beyond my resources.

The next step was to teach networking. Though I had been teaching Sam all along in our cell, he had finally been allowed to attend the classes when one of the inmates made parole. He took to networking like a duck to water. I decided to split the class in half, with each half being a network. I was able to persuade the warden to get me a used router since they could be had for next to nothing, and a bunch of networking cable, and began to teach networking.

First, we started with the cabling, and the differences in the cables that were used, and why certain ones were used in which situation. Basically, the way I learned about networking, from the ground up so that's how I taught it. Then we went on to protocols and their role, graduating on to installation and troubleshooting. All of this took months since we only had two hours a day. My students could be found in the common areas talking about computers, software, networking, and anything else to do with computers, much to the amusement of other inmates. They became known as the Geek Squad, and they must have considered it a badge of honour. For the most part, the other inmates left us alone, since we might have been talking Latin for all they could figure out.

Chapter 4

I was finally released from prison, having served a full seven years. Sam had been released about two months before me, and his replacement didn't know anything about " 'puters and geek stuff, and didn't want to know." We agreed to disagree. Except for Sam being gone, not much really changed for me. I got the call to the wardens' office and informed of my impending release.

We had not become friends, that wouldn't ever happen, but we had a mutual respect. I told him that I could never repay him for the trust he had in me, and the chances he had given me while in prison. His response almost moved me to tears for the first time in this place.

"Mike, I've seen hundreds of men come through these doors and could count on two hands the number that I thought would be able to flourish on the outside. You're one of the few. Your behaviour in here was exemplary, and it was almost a pleasure seeing you develop into a responsible young man. I know that you have a great future ahead of you, and the only thanks you can give is to get back into the world and become the best that you can be. "

I was somewhat stunned at this coming from the warden, but what he said next really floored me. "You have served a full seven years, including the one year in the hospital. You will be on parole for 3 years after your release. Here are the terms of your parole. Read and heed is the only advice I can give you. Do you have anywhere to live when you get out?"

"Uh, I don't, um it's...No sir, but I didn't expect this. I guess I have to make some phone calls if I have permission."

"Granted. Officer, escort Mr Foster to the visiting area and let him make his phone calls. Mike, your release is scheduled for next week. Good luck. I don't expect to see you back here again."

"Thank you, sir, I'll do my best not to let you down, or me."

So I was released. My youngest sister, Debra, told me that I could bunk at their place until I got things arranged. She and her husband (it didn't seem that long, but my youngest sister was married?) had a spare room in their basement that I could use. She met me in the visitors' parking lot with a huge hug and chattered non-stop for the four hours it took to get to her house.

Gerry, her husband, wouldn't be home until around 5:00, so I could just relax and enjoy my first day of freedom. I didn't really want to go anywhere, and quite happily sat in the sun in their backyard, playing with George, their very spoiled Shih Tsu. I became his new best friend because I would play throw the ball as long as he wanted.

Debra came out and told me she had to run to the store, and did I need anything. I told her I was good and I and George would stay and guard the house. She giggled since George was curled up in a ball on the foot of my chaise lounge, sound asleep, tired from his game of chase the ball. I had an ice tea going, and was just enjoying the peace and quiet.

I must have dozed off, because the next voice I heard was my brother, Jimmy. "Hey, you. You're lookin' good. Glad you're out. I thought we'd hang out a bit. My boss gave me some time off. He knows all about you." He continued on in this vein for a while, and we gradually got caught up on our lives. He was the assistant manager of an auto parts store and looked to have a good future with them.

His girlfriend was a dental assistant and would be over when she was finished work. Lori, my other sister, and her significant other would be over later as well. The only one missing would be Mom; she couldn't get here until tomorrow and would be staying with Lori.

Debra got home and started to get some things together for dinner. Jimmy appointed himself the Lorieque chef and was happily burning meat when Gerry came home from work. He greeted me warmly and said he glad to finally meet the oldest brother.

The fact that I had just got out of prison never came up at all. As a matter of fact, we began discussing computers and how they could be adapted to help run his business, an office supply company. He had several large contracts and badly needed some help with all the paperwork. It gave me something to think about.

Lori and her partner Brenda arrived not too long after Gerry. I was a bit surprised at the relationship but if they were happy, that was alright with me. They were a bit guarded around me at first, understandably, but soon realized that I certainly wasn't going to judge them. We then all sat down together to eat, me with George at my feet looking for handouts, and it became just a family gathering with lots of laughing, teasing and gossip. It was good to be out. I didn't realize how much I'd missed my siblings.

Later, after everyone left, I asked Debra if it was okay to have a shower. She laughed and said that no permission was needed. Old habits die hard. I was used to only one shower a week. A bath would have been an untold luxury. I felt really tired and went to bed shortly after my shower.

I thought that I would sleep like a baby. Not a chance. The bed was too comfortable and the house too quiet. Even during quiet hours, prisons are a noisy place. I guess it would take time to get used to my new life. After all, it hadn't even been one day yet.

Giving up on sleep, I quietly went to the kitchen and got some more iced tea, then went and sat outside on the deck. It was a beautiful night. No moon and the stars seemed to be extra bright just because I was free. I began thinking of what kind of program would be best for Gerry. I wasn't sure exactly what paperwork he was talking about so I ran several scenarios over in my mind. I was sure that I could work something out, or even adopt a current commercial product to suit his needs. It was something to explore in the days ahead.

Late the next morning, after some breakfast and the luxury of another shower, I took the bus downtown. I knew that I still had some money on deposit in the Credit Union I'd dealt with while I was in university. I just didn't know how much. I was pleasantly surprised to find over $5,000 in my account. I asked the teller if I could get up to date statements going back almost eight years. She had to call her manager to help with that, and I was greeted like a long lost friend by an acquaintance from the university. He had been in a different program, but we had shared a couple of classes.

He invited me into his office while one of the staff got the statements for me. I took the opportunity to ask about business financing and what they would need for me to set up an account. Since I did get my degree while in prison, I thought about setting up a small shop that dealt with computer repair and small business networking.

I wouldn't need a lot of capital to start, and I could approach some suppliers about pricing and financing. Fred, the manager, told me that I shouldn't rush into getting a bunch of financing at the start. Get the business up and running then expand slowly. I thought that this was good advice on his part and thanked him as I grabbed all the statements and headed back to Debra's house.

So now I had two projects, find a place to live, and find a place to set up shop. Another thing I had to decide is where, exactly, that this new life would take place. I had decided at my Dad's funeral that moving back to the old home town wasn't an option.

I had Debra take me to Fairview to meet my parole officer, Tim Simpson, who turned out to be a decent guy. I asked if I could get permission to move to Kent, a town of about 20,000 people almost midway between my hometown of Bridgeville and the university located in Fairview. When I explained my plans to him, he was all for it. I would still have to drive into Fairview to meet him, but I didn't think this would be a problem.

My next self-appointed task was to find an affordable set of wheels so that I was mobile. I also got permission for that, though I really didn't need it. I thought that I might have to take a driving test, or at least a refresher course. He thought that might be a good idea, but I could play it by ear.

I got back to Debra's just in time for lunch. While we were eating I explained my plans to her. Although it was only my second day free, it seemed like longer since things seemed to be going my way for a change. We got into her Subaru and went vehicle shopping. Since I would have a store, what I needed had to be large enough for carrying boxes and stuff, but economical. I ended up settling on an older Ford Ranger extended cab. It was in my price range and would have to do for now.

We then drove over to Kent to see about apartments and store spaces for rent. The apartment was fairly easy, and we found a two-bedroom not too far from the downtown core. One bedroom would be set up as an office. Finding an appropriate and affordable store for rent was more problematic. There were quite a few for rent, but you'd have thought it was downtown Vancouver for what they wanted.

I could see why they were vacant. We ended up talking to a property manager who was an acquaintance of Debra and Gerry, and once again, luck was on my side. An older widow had just closed her sweet shop. The other half of the building was a coffee shop that also served breakfast and lunch. It was open until 4:00 each afternoon, and closed weekends. The half that she wanted to rent was a perfect size.

Over coffee, I discovered that her ultimate goal was to sell the whole building and move to the coast to be closer to her grandkids. This was, apparently, a five-year plan. We ultimately came to a deal where I would have right of first refusal to buy the whole building if things worked out for me.

I would be responsible for utilities and the like but would get a discount on meals and coffee. A handshake sealed the deal, and we left the property manager to get the paperwork ready. Mary was a real sweetheart and I had a feeling that we would become friends. Later I would realize that she was almost like a second mother.

Everything was going so well, and so quickly, that I wondered if it were some kind of weird dream. Given my past, I was wondering when the roof would cave in. Debra phoned our Mom who said she would be there for dinner, and yes I could have my old bedroom set and a few other things from the house. She was planning to sell the house anyway, so it would be just that much less that she'd have to get rid of.

I took the rest of the afternoon to relax and play with George. Maybe, just maybe, my life was getting back on track. It was too early to tell, of course, but things were definitely looking up.

Chapter 5

The next few weeks were hectic, but finally, I was in my apartment and the store was almost ready for opening. I just had to wait for the various governments to give their approval, and I could open. Gerry, with his business contacts, was an invaluable resource. I found him to be a great guy and perfect for my little sister. Instead of just brothers in law, we were becoming buddies.

I was messing around in the store, getting the work area organized and puttering around when the chime sounded, advising that someone had come into the store. The monitor from the security camera showed that a woman had come in and was looking around. I went out front and said, "I'm sorry ma'am, I'm not open for..." and realized it was my sister Lori.

"Mike, I just thought I'd pop in and see how it's going. Debra said that you're nearly ready to open."

"Yeah, just waiting for the bureaucrats, you know how slow they can be. But, I'm good at waiting. If nothing else, I did learn that inside."

"Don't sell yourself short. From what I've heard you did a lot more than that. Never thought that my big brother would become a teacher."

"Who have you been talking to?"

"Mike, your parole officer is Mandy's brother. He and his wife were over at our place the other night and I asked about you. He thinks very highly of you, even though you've only met once. Of course, I couldn't see it, but I guess the report from the prison was a real eye-opener."

"Yeah, well. I just tried to keep busy until my time was up."

"Just keep thinking that, big brother," she laughed, punching me lightly on the arm. "Come on and let's go get a coffee. " We went next door to Mary's and settled in at a table near the back. Mary came over with the coffees and profusely thanked me for setting up internet access in the cafe. She'd always wanted to do it but thought it would cost too much and take too long. It had taken me about 2 hours using some used parts. I told her it would cost her a lunch someday.

"Mike," said Lori, "I'm not really sure how to bring this up." She took a huge breath, slowly exhaling, then continued, "It's about Lynsy, I thought..."

"Don't even go there Lori." I became angry, really angry. What was this with her bringing up Lynsy? That water was long under the bridge. "As far as she goes, she doesn't exist in my world, and won't! Ever! That subject is taboo and it's not negotiable."

"I knew you'd feel that way." She placed her hand over mine and squeezed gently. "Mike, I don't blame you one bit, but please hear me out." I sat there for a moment, feeling my guts twisting again as the last seven years of my life flashed across my brain. No, not gonna happen. I didn't want to hear about her and certainly didn't want to see or talk to her.

"Sorry, Lori. No. There's too much baggage there. That's one subject that's off the table"

"But Mike, I just want to..."

"No Lori, anything but that. And that's final. I've spent over seven years getting her out of my system, so, no, I don't even want to hear her name." She nodded, accepting the finality of my statement. We chatted on about other things, but the black cloud that had settled over me wouldn't go away. After a while she rose to go, "I have to get back. Mandy and I have some things to do." She gave me a quick peck on the cheek and was gone.

I went back to the shop, but couldn't concentrate on getting anything done, not that there was much to do anyway. I decided that I needed someone to talk to, someone who could give me an objective viewpoint or at least understand what I was thinking. Sam, my ex-cellmate. Of course! I had tracked him down to a suburb of Vancouver. I didn't know if he was working or what but resolved to give him a call after dinner.

"Sam, it's Mike. How's it going? Finally tracked you down. What made you move to the coast?"

"Mike, man. Good to hear a friendly voice. Things aren't too good. I'm at my parents' place right now, living in their granny suite in the basement. Not much work out there for a big, black ex-con computer guy."

"Sam, I'm really sorry to hear that. Really. I didn't even bother with that part. I decided that after seven years of being ordered around, I wanted to be the boss for a change. Started up my own place. Grand opening probably in a week or so once all the paperwork is done."

"Glad for you man. If I could afford it I'd look at doing that too. Costs an arm and two legs just to find a closet down here. My parents offered to help me out, but they'd be just pouring money down the drain. Fuck, man. I'm almost at an end. Don't know what to do. I do want to do the computer thing, but it's not putting any food on the table."

We chatted on for a few minutes. A germ of an idea came to me. Sam was a friend, and he'd be great in the store. "Sam, I've got an idea. Give me tonight to work on it and I'll call you tomorrow. You going to be at this number?" I had forgotten the original reason for my call.

"Yeah, I'll be here. Nowhere else to go right now. What are you thinkin' man?"

"Later. I'll call tomorrow and let you know if this works out. I don't want to get your hopes up, but really, I do have an idea."

"Okay man. Thanks for calling. Good to hear from you. Talk to you tomorrow."

"Bye Sam." I made a couple of phone calls. The others I'd make in the morning. The huge black cloud had lifted somewhat. I'd be helping myself and a buddy at the same time.

Next morning I was on the phone to the Credit Union manager. I explained to him my plan. He said that he could see no problem as far as they were concerned. Then I called my parole officer. I didn't know what he'd think of my plan, or if he'd want the extra workload. I got an appointment for that afternoon and went over to Fairview to run my plan by him.

"What I'm thinking of doing is bringing a friend in to help with my business. Problem is, he's an ex-con, same as me. Right now he's down at the coast, but I know he'd move up here if there was an opportunity for him. I gotta tell you, he's the biggest black guy I've ever met. We were cellmates and he was one of my students in that computer class I ran. He took to it like a duck to water, and I know we'd do well together."

"Okay, Mike. Give me the details," and I went on to explain what I was planning. "Okay, Mike this sounds pretty good. Let me make a couple of calls and get back to you. Do you know who his parole officer is?"

"Nope, but I can find out."

"Never mind. I can get the info off our database. You going to be home or at the store later?"

"I'll be at the store until around 5:00, then at home."

"Sounds good. I'll let you know one way or the other later today."

"That's all I can ask. I appreciate it." I almost danced out of his office, got into my little truck and went running some errands. I stopped in to see Gerry and get more details about what he needed for that computer program I was looking at designing for him. Over coffee, we discussed several options and came to the decision that adapting an existing program would be the way to go. I told him I'd spec out a few and see about getting a developers licence.

I headed back to my store and waited for the phone to ring. I still wasn't open, but there were things I could do. If nothing else, I could dream. I went next door, got a coffee and a sandwich to go, talked to Mary for a few minutes, and went back to the store. The phone was ringing when I got there.

"Mike, Tim Simpson."

"Yes, Mr Simpson."

"Please, it's Tim."

"Okay, Mr Simp...I mean Tim."

"Here's what you need to do..." and he filled me in on all the details of what Sam would need. My next call was to Sam. I could almost feel his change of attitude over the phone when I explained to him the plan and what he needed. My biggest concern, for him and me, was being self-sufficient until the business could support us. I was hoping for six months, but expecting longer. I was lucky in that Gerry had given me a retainer towards his program, and I still had some of my $5,000 left. If all went well, Sam would be working with me in about a month. He was over the moon.

I talked to my landlord and found that she had a vacancy on the second floor. It was only a one bedroom, but it would have to do. I put a hold on it on Sam's behalf. It was coming together. Soon I'd have a buddy working with me. When Sam got here, we'd have to think up a new business name, but that was for the future.

The next few weeks were hectic. I'd finally got all the government paperwork, and did open the doors. There was no big grand opening, just an advertisement in the local paper stating that a new computer service centre was open for business. I was busier than I thought I'd be at the start. The good thing was that I was able to solve every problem the customers brought in. I didn't feel that charging Vancouver rates was warranted in this town, and I was right. Word got around that I was good and, more importantly, affordable.

Right on schedule, Sam arrived on the Greyhound. We had a great reunion and happily chatted long into the night. He'd be bunking with me until his apartment was ready in a few days. Meanwhile, he'd have to get squared away with the parole officer and get ready for moving into his apartment. He'd start in the store the following Monday.

I called Debra and asked if I could bring a friend to the weekly Lorieque on Saturday. I told her I'd bring the wine and potato salad. She said she'd put on an extra steak. I grinned and wondered what she would think when she saw the size of my guest. I was fairly certain she was expecting female company.

My poor little truck struggled all the way to Fairview. Sam was so big that he could hardly fit into the cab. All he talked about on our short trip was getting some real wheels, meaning a vehicle big enough for him to fit in. We arrived at Debra and Gerry's, and I noticed that Lori and Mandy were already there. I saw Jimmy pull in behind me. His girlfriend wasn't with him. We later learned that he had caught her with another guy. Could I ever relate to that!

Debra warmly greeted Sam. The look on her face when I brought Sam around back was priceless, but if he was a friend of her big brother, he must be okay. Lori and Mandy were reclined on some chaise lounges and got up to welcome Sam as well. Gerry spoke for all of them when he came out of the house, "Christ almighty, I need more than one extra steak!" and with the ice broken by everyone cracking up, we settled easily into the weekly Lorieque. As time went on, Sam would be a frequent and welcome guest, and even bring his date and future wife with him once in a while.

Monday, Sam walked with me to the store. I took him over and introduced him to Mary. She welcomed him warmly and said that the same discount I enjoyed would apply to him as well. We opened up and got to work. I'd had several repair jobs come in late on Friday, and promised to have them ready today. As I expected, Sam was great with the customers. If you didn't know better, you'd never guess that he had killed a man. Well, I guess that applied to me as well. It was something that had happened, we'd served our time and all that was behind us.

Over the next several months we got really busy. Our store was becoming well known for good service and reasonable rates. Word of mouth was great advertising. Sam was a better front counter man than me, so he did most of the storefront stuff. I worked on developing major contracts. We both did repairs in the back. It got so busy that after some discussion we decided we needed to hire some staff. We decided that we'd hire someone to help look after the front counter, and get someone to help in the back, preferably a student who was going to major in computer science.

The choices weren't easy. We had quite a few applicants for both positions. The first student we hired for the repair shop tuned out to be our landlord's nephew. Mary hadn't talked to us but had told him to apply. Kevin turned out to be a good kid, and fitted in and worked well. Mary was really happy about that since she had never mentioned him to us, so there was never any pressure.

We ended up going through five different people for the front counter work. We had to be able to trust them, and they had to be willing to learn. We ended up hiring a young woman, about 25 years old. She was part Jamaican, part white and, I thought, quite pretty. It turned out that she had had several jobs but was let go when businesses were downsizing; just an unfortunate luck of the draw. However, we were expanding and hoped to do so for the foreseeable future.

Her husband had been killed over in Afghanistan, one of the first of many that died there, and she was trying to raise 2 kids on her survivor's pension and what little money she could earn from various small jobs. We were happy to have her on board and found Sonia to be a really nice person, hard worker, and really good with the public.

Sam and I were both pleasantly surprised to find that if she didn't know about something, she wouldn't hesitate to ask. The others tried to bullshit their way through it, doing themselves and the business a disservice. I was happy that the business was doing well but I still had a nagging feeling that something was missing.

Chapter 6

Lynsy Tells Her Side

My name is Lynsy Brown. This is how I totally fucked up my life. I'm not a raving beauty or centrefold type, just a girl-next-door. Like Mike, I guess I'm just average, which is necessarily a bad thing. I'm not the big, busty blond who spreads her legs for anyone. I'm only about 5'2" and weigh in at 105 lb on a good day. My breasts aren't huge, little more than a handful. Mike always said that size didn't matter.

Mike and I had grown up together and had been best friends forever. We became lovers when he graduated from high school. Everyone expected that LM, as we were known, would become a couple and eventually marry. I followed Mike to university the next year after graduating. I'd talked my Dad into letting me rent an apartment instead of living in dorms.

The thought of becoming one of those "sorority" types turned me cold, and I was quite happy being independent in my own apartment. Mike was a regular visitor, of course, and you'd think we were a married couple some of the time. I especially liked it when I got home Friday after classes to find dinner in the oven, and wine chilling in the fridge. Mike could cook, probably as well as I could, so meals were good and varied, and our love life was fantastic.

During the first year, we were totally monogamous. We had a large circle of friends, both geeks on his side, and the scientists (nerds) on mine. We were having a great time, and even during the summer breaks, we were mostly together. We both had summer jobs, he in computers of course, and I worked in the rec centre. Life was good, and I was happy. So was Mike. We were in love and everyone could tell.

Things changed at the start of my second year and his third. Mike and I had only one class together, English since he was in the computer science curriculum. Our class schedules didn't allow us a lot of time together, though we were together in my apartment a couple of times a week in the evening, and of course on weekends. Our social life was pretty much as it had been in other years, mostly going out with friends on Saturdays.

There was a new guy in most of my classes named Todd. He had transferred from another school back east. I won't go into the details, but he seduced me and I went along. Somehow I justified it that since Todd was so totally different than Mike, and it was just sex, that the fact I was cheating wouldn't matter too much. Of course, I knew that it would hurt Mike if he ever found out, but I honestly didn't think it would happen. I expected Todd to be a short-term thing. It's funny how we can justify our mistakes.

We would meet, usually, first thing Mondays in my apartment since that was the time we were both free from classes. I had told Mike that I had classes, as did he, on Mondays so he usually went back to his dorm Sunday night. Todd and I would fuck in the morning, then he would leave and I'd get ready for my afternoon classes. Todd wanted more, but I had told him we were just "friends with benefits", and Mike was my man.

Then came that terrible, terrible day. To this day I don't know how Mike found out. As usual, Todd and I were in the bedroom having sex. He had this scenario that played out the same every week. The sex would last for an hour or so then Todd would get dressed and leave. I'm pretty sure that we were never seen together.

Anyway, Todd left and I had a shower and got dressed for school. I was going into the kitchen to make some lunch when I saw the photo of me and Mike on the table beside my books. The heavy black X across the glass imploded my world. My first thought was to call Mike. I grabbed my phone then noticed the key to my apartment on the floor. Now I was Leahtic. I called his cell but went to voicemail. I called his room phone. There was no answer; it went to the answering machine. I went into the second bedroom that served as sort of an office and saw that his computer and all the software disks were gone. Now I knew for sure, he must have seen Todd and me.

After trying to reach Mike, I phoned Todd and told him we were through, and that Mike had somehow found out about us. Yes, the sex was good, but that was all. I would never see him again except in class. Being a typical selfish jock, his reasoning was that since Mike and I would no longer be together, we could hook up officially. I hung up on him and continued to call Mike. At least I was able to get his answering machine, and I left about ten messages, basically all saying the same thing. He never did call me back.

I didn't attend classes that afternoon, nor the next day. I knew that Mike sometimes went for a run in the afternoon, and even knew his route. I left the apartment just after 3:00 and jogged from the apartment building to where I knew Mike ran. My heart leapt as I saw Mike loping along about 300 metres in front of me. I sped up, trying to catch up to him. I saw him glance over his shoulder and briefly stumble, then dart across the street, dodging traffic. I wasn't able to follow right away, and by the time I got across the street, he was gone.

Defeated, I walked slowly back to my apartment. I saw one of the students, Leah Brown, from my English class approaching. I didn't really know her, just who she was. I think she was in Mikes' program, but I wasn't sure. As she got to me, she spoke, "Lynsy?"

"Yes?"

Then she hit me. It was just an open hand slap across my face. Then she hit me again, with the other hand. "What were you thinking you, stupid whore? Mike's one of the good guys on campus and you had to cheat on him. You stupid bitch! Do you have any idea what you've done? Do you know how devastated he his? It's a good thing I don't believe in violence. I should kick the shit out of you!"

"I, I didn't..."

"What? Think? No shit Einstein. Where was your fucking brain? In your cunt along with Todd's cock? You make me sick to my stomach. When the word gets out you'll be lucky to have even one friend left on this campus. And you deserve it. Bitch!"

"Leah, do you know...?"

"Don't fucking talk to me, ever. Whatever happens, you don't deserve Mike, and he sure doesn't deserve someone like you!" Leah yelled at me then stomped off toward her dorm. I didn't know how she knew, or what she knew, but I guess it was enough. I slowly made my way back to my apartment, resolving along the way to get together with Mike and explain.

Maybe we wouldn't be together, but at least he wouldn't hate me. I spent the rest of the week and part of the next trying to get hold of him. He wouldn't answer my calls, and Ed, his roommate would never tell me if he was there. I tried the computer labs and even the data centre where he worked, all without success. He had locked me out of his world.

I thought that I might see him at least in the English class we shared, but I found out that he had changed his schedule. We would have no classes together. I also noticed that classmates who had been friends that we hung out with were civil towards me, but certainly not friendly like before. The words that Leah had said came back to me. I knew what she had said was coming true. My world, as I knew it, was ending.

It was a lonely semester. Classmates only talked to me when they had to for group projects. I asked one of them, Jill, who I knew only slightly if this was because of Mike. She said, "Lynsy, you really fucked this one up. Mike is highly thought of on this campus. You know that he tutors other students who need help?"

I nodded yes.

"Well, almost everyone in our class has needed his help or knows someone who needed it. Even your lover Todd was getting tutoring from him. He never even charged for the ones that couldn't really afford it. You just sucked the life right out of him. Everyone can see it but you. You were just so intent on getting tail, you never even thought of him. The people in this class will probably never forgive you for that. I know I won't." With that, Jill turned around and walked away.

I didn't realize just how well thought of he was because he never, ever blew his own trumpet. It just wasn't his nature. It had never occurred to me that my actions affected more than just the three of us. It was a revelation just how selfish and childish I'd been. As was the revelation that Todd was getting tutoring from him. Neither had mentioned it. Of course, that wouldn't be happening now. I resigned myself to finishing the semester, then leaving this school. There was no way I could finish my studies here.

I advised my parents that I was leaving school at the end of the semester, and would try to find another school. I refused to go into detail, telling them that we'd talk when I got home at the end of the semester. I would be home about a week before Christmas.

As soon as I walked in the door of my home, I knew that they knew what I had done. To my surprise, there was no yelling or screaming, which I would have deserved. My Dad wouldn't talk to me at all and my Mom just said, "How could you?" She would only answer a direct question with a "yes" or "no" and refused to have much to do with me. Her kitchen, where I'd hung out for hours laughing and talking with her, was now out of bounds except for eating.

My brother was overseas and wouldn't be home for another year. Unless someone told him, he wouldn't know the story, at least until he got home. For that I was grateful. The day after I got home, Mom sat me down in the kitchen. Dad was at work and wouldn't be home for a couple of hours. "Lynsy, we need to talk. I only found out about you from Mike's mother. He isn't coming home for Christmas and told her something had happened. He wouldn't say what, just that something had happened between you, and if we wanted to find out, to ask you. What happened?"

I broke down, and between sobs, related the whole story, assigning blame where it clearly belonged, right on my shoulders. She didn't interrupt as I spoke, just sitting there stone-faced as I talked. At the end, she simply said, "If you weren't my daughter whom I love dearly, I'd kick your ass out that door quick as you can say. What on earth were you thinking girl? Or were you even thinking? Mikes' mother is going to be devastated when you tell her, and you WILL be telling her.

We're going over there in about ten minutes. Go get cleaned up." There was no give in her at all. I'd arrived in Purgatory. We weren't aware of the events unfolding back at the university at almost exactly this same time. I wish I had been, though I have no idea what I would have done.

We went over to the Fosters and found his sisters and mother there. His brother was out with his latest girlfriend. To say it was unpleasant is an understatement. I again related what I had done and how the ramifications were now coming home to roost. After I finished talking, Mom hugged the three women and we returned home. We were all bawling, but I was ignored. The two girls, who I had grown up with looked at me with absolute disgust on their face.

My Dad spoke to me a couple of days later, the first time since I'd returned from college. "Lynsy, if you weren't my daughter, I'd disown you. As it is, you are my daughter, and I and your mother do love you. We hate what you have done to our two families, but you are our daughter and we'll support you within reason. This is what's going to happen in the New Year," and he related to me how he had made a few phone calls and asked for some favours. I would be finishing my courses at BCIT near Vancouver.

Dad would help with my tuition, but I was expected to get and keep a job for other living expenses. I wouldn't have my car and would be staying with an Aunt not too far from campus. I would be expected to be working and studying, and forget about a social life. I had 2 ½ years of courses left but I would be finished in 1 ½ years because I would be going year round. My grades had better be good, or the support I was receiving would end.

There was no discussing the matter. My Dad had made the arrangements, and if I didn't like it, I would be out of the house and on my own. New Years Day found me on a Greyhound headed to Vancouver. My Aunt Maddy would pick me up at the depot and take me to her place in Burnaby. I'd have two days to get settled and find a job.

And so it went. I got a job in a local restaurant. I did nothing but study and work. Sunday was my day off and I'd usually go to church with my Aunt, afterwards reading or watching TV. She did drag me around on various outings to the park, or an art gallery, or something like that, telling me that I had to get out more.

I didn't know if she knew the story about Mike and me, so I sat down one evening and asked her. To my surprise, she knew the whole story and had even talked to Mike's mother. No, he didn't hate me, but no, he wouldn't talk to me either. I never did hear about Mike killing Todd and going to prison until months later after I graduated.

My Aunt then went on to explain that she wouldn't judge me. She knew what I had done, and knew that I had taken responsibility for the whole thing. Part of the reason was her background. When she was young she had done something similar but went so far as to move in with the guy she cheated with. At that time, living in sin was the ultimate insult to her family, and they pretty much disowned her.

Some months later she came to realize that this guy was a huge mistake. He wasn't looking for a partner, he wanted a substitute mother to wait on him hand and foot, and do what he wanted when he wanted. Maddy moved out and had been mostly on her own since then. Yes, she'd had boyfriends, but she always measured them against her first, true love, and they came up lacking.

He had moved on and, several years after Maddy had left him, married a wonderful girl. They have four kids, and Maddy sees the family often. The kids think of her as an aunt, though they're not related. She often wonders about what could have been but knows that it won't happen. And, no, she wouldn't tell me who it was.

I graduated 18 months after I'd started from BCIT, just as my Dad had said. Because of my grades, the class wanted me to be valedictorian. I declined. They were classmates, but not friends since I had no social life, and had never been to any class functions. My parents, brother Rob and Aunt Maddy were there to see me graduate. Afterwards, we went out to a fancy restaurant for a celebratory dinner. For the first time in two years, I felt, if not happy, then at least satisfied that I had accomplished something.

I moved back to the hometown and went to work for one of the medical laboratories in Fairview. Eventually, I found an apartment not too far from work which saved on commuting time. Since they did quite a lot of work for several clinics not only in Fairview but for Kent and Bridgeville as well, it was a busy place.

It was there that I met Mike's sister Lori. She had come into the lab for some routine blood work and I was assigned to do the job. I went into the room without knowing ahead of time who I'd be dealing with and saw her sitting patiently waiting for me. It was all I could do to close the door and sit down at the desk.

"Hello Lori, how can I help you," I asked. "Do you have your requisition?"

"Lynsy, what are you doing here? I never knew you were back in town."

"Let's just say that I don't go out much. I started here a couple of months ago. How is Mike?"

"How is Ev...you don't know, do you?"

"Don't know what? Is he okay, did he finally move on?" I asked.

"He's in prison for killing your lover."

I heard the words and collapsed. The next thing I remember is waking up in the hospital with a very worried mother sitting beside the bed.

"Mom, where am I, what am I doing here? What's going on?"

"Settle down Lynsy. I'll let the nurse know that you're awake. You passed out at work and your boss had the ambulance bring you here. Since I'm your next of kin, they called me." Then I remembered. Lori. Mike is in prison. I hadn't known. "Mom, did you know about Mike being in prison?"

"Yes, I sat through most of his trial with his parents. They took it really hard."

"Can you tell me what happened?"

"I can only tell you the part that I heard in court. I visit Syl (Mikes' mother) quite often, but that is one subject that is never brought up, ever. She thinks that Mike being in prison contributed to his Dad's death, and I'm inclined to agree. However, she doesn't hold you responsible, and neither does Mike. It was just a tragic mistake."

She then went on to relate what had happened in the dorm room and how Todd had gotten shot. I held it together until she finished, then totally lost it. The doctor came in, saw I was hystLynsyl and gave me a sedative which knocked me out right away. I was out for nearly 20 hours.

I was released from the hospital two days later and moved in with my parents for a week at the insistence of my mother. I was totally numb with shock over the whole matter. I went back to my apartment on the Sunday and back to work Monday morning. I still had a hard time believing everything I'd heard. Mike killed someone? There had to be more to the story. Maybe I'd be able to find out from Lori.

Chapter 7

We'd been open a year. Sam and Sonia worked mostly in the front of the store, while I worked with the businesses that had accounts with us, and did all the paperwork. I had Kevin and another young guy doing the repairs in the workshop in the back. I was in my office one afternoon doing said paperwork when Sonia knocked and came into the office, closing the door behind her. I knew it wasn't a social call because I had made it clear that I don't date staff, ever. What they did with their private lives was up to them.

"Mike, can I talk to you? It's about Sam."

"Sam? What's he done?" This worried me. We were both still on parole and couldn't take a chance of any problems in our lives. So far parole had been good and neither of us had done anything to jeopardize it.

"Nothing. That's the problem?"

"Twice again, please. In English."

"Mike, I really like Sam, and would like to have a chance for a relationship with him."

"Um, Sonia, this is way out of my area of expertise. Why don't you just tell him?"

"Oh we chat and joke around, but he acts more like I'm a younger sister or co-worker, not a friend. My upbringing doesn't really allow me to approach him. I'm old fashioned that way. But if he were to ask..."

"So you want me to talk to Sam for you?"

"Well, sort of. Just maybe let him know that if he asks, the response would probably be positive. I know you won't date employees. Does that apply to Sam, too?"

"No, that's not a company policy, that's just my policy and it applies just to me. I'll talk to him, but if he asks, we never had this conversation."

"Thanks so much, Mike. I'll really, really appreciate it," and with that, she left my office, a huge smile on her face. Now, how the hell was I going to approach Sam? Well, that would have to wait. He was on a job over in Fairview and wouldn't be back until after the store closed.

After dinner, I was relaxing in front of the tube with an iced tea when Sam knocked on the door and came into my apartment. "Just getting in?" I asked. "No man, I stopped for supper on the way. No sense trying to eat my own cookin'," he laughed. It was well known his idea of gourmet was a couple of fully loaded cheeseburgers. "I wanted to ask you about something, but didn't want to do it in the store."

"Sounds serious. You in trouble? You want something to drink?"

"No, nothing like that. Yeah, ice tea sounds good since you probably don't have any beer. It's just that you have this policy about dating employees..." I got up to go get his iced tea. As he took a large gulp I said, "Sam, that policy only applies to me. What all you guys do is up to you as long as it doesn't in any way affect the business. Why you wanna date Sonia?"

"How did you know?"

"Just a wild guess since she's the only woman on staff," I laughed at him. "So what's the problem? Go ask her out."

"Yeah, well. I thought that policy..."

"Come on Sam, you knew that was my policy, but just for me. Anyway, go ahead and ask her. All I ask is that you go easy. She's had a pretty rough go of it. Does she know about your, I mean our, past?"

"Yeah. She knows your sister and got it out of her."

"Which one? My sisters have big mouths?"

"I m not going to say. So you're okay with this? I mean Sonia?"

"Yeah man, I'd never stand in the way of true love."

He finished his drink and started out the door. "You know Mike, you're standing in your own way. Will, you ever get over her?"

"Lynsy?" I grimaced since his words were sort of echoing my feelings. "I don't know man. I don't even know if she's dead or alive or even where she is."

"Well, Bro, I know all that stuff. If you need to know, just ask." And with that, he closed the door and went back to his own place before I could answer. What the hell? How is it that everyone seems to know what's going on in my life except me? I decided to phone Debra since she had met Sam first, and he was a frequent guest at the Saturday Lorieque at her house.

"Hi, Sis. What's up?"

"Mike, Gerry was just talking about you. Seems you might have to come over and expand his program again. Since you set it up sales have started going nuts. He just got home."

"Sis, have you been talking to Sam?"

"Not other than at the Lorieques. Should I? I know he's talked to Lori and Mandy a few times. I assumed it was about parole and stuff since Mandy's brother is your parole officer. Why, what's going on?"

"Do you know Sonia from the shop?"

"Just to see her. She seems nice. Why, is there trouble?"

"Not yet. There could be if those two become an item. Sam wanted my blessing to ask her for a date."

"I don't understand. Why would he need your blessing?" She seemed genuinely puzzled. "Well, I have this policy about not dating employees. He seemed to think it applied to everyone, but it's only for me. The others can do what they want as long as the business isn't affected. So, in a sense, I guess I gave him my blessing. I thought that he got all the info about her from you since you're about the same age as Sonia, and he's over to your place often enough."

"It wasn't me, it must have been Lori and Mandy. I'm pretty sure they know her from where she used to work, and I know Lori's talked to her in your store. I hope she and Sam get together. I like him. He's like that huge teddy bear I've always wanted. And he's a nice guy."

"Yeah, that he is." We talked for a few more minutes then I ended the call. So, Lori and Mandy. Now I wasn't sure how to handle this or even approach them. They had information about Lynsy. To be honest, deep down I'd never gotten over her, even after all that happened.

I called their house and Mandy answered, "Mike, a pleasant surprise. What's up?"

"Hi, Mandy. I just wondered if you two would like to do lunch tomorrow. I've got some things I want to run by you."

"Yeah, sure Mike. I'll let Lori know. She's over at the neighbours right now going over some decorating ideas."

"Great, I'll pick you up at 12 Noon. Don't be late," I laughed as I hung up. The next day I pulled up in front of Lori and Mandy's home decorating business just as they were coming out and locking the door. They both jumped into my truck and I drove down to one of the few really good family restaurants in town.

Once we were settled at the table and had placed our orders, I started, "Okay you two. What have you been telling people about me and Sam? Me I don't care, but Sam's got a chance to make a real life for himself and I don't want it screwed up."

Lori looked at Mandy, who looked back at Lori. Mandy began, "Okay, you got us. I got some info from my brother, your parole officer. I know he's not supposed to talk about his "clients" but we, us and Meg, his wife, ganged up on him so he gave us a brief outline on both of you. He thinks you guys have your shit together, or he probably wouldn't have said anything."

"Did you tell Sonia about us?" I asked. "Yeah, we saw her in the supermarket one day and she asked if we knew anything about Sam. So we went and had a coffee and told her what we knew. We wouldn't lie about it," said Mandy.

Lori continued, "We just told her what we had been told. You both did time for manslaughter, you're both on parole, and your parole officer says you've got it together. Honest Mike, we didn't say anything else."

"Okay, you two, not to worry. It's just that yesterday I had Sonia come in and ask about dating Sam and then last night he came by my apartment to ask about dating Sonia. I told them that it's none of my business who they dated as long as it doesn't affect the business. I also asked him if she knew about his background. He said that she did, and she'd got it from one of my sisters. I thought it might have been Debra since she's about the same age as Sonia. I called her, and she spilt the beans," I ended with a laugh.

Our lunches came and general talk continued through lunch. The server cleared the plates away and refilled our coffees. Lori glanced at Mandy, who nodded. Oh, oh, I thought, something's was up.

"Mike, I know you said that this is a taboo subject," Lori started.

"Lynsy."

"Yes. You won't talk about her and you won't talk to her. I've run into her a couple of times. She asks about you all the time."

"So? When did she get this sudden urge to ask about a killer?"

"Mike, that's uncalled for. She's just as hurt as you about the whole matter. She didn't even know you were in prison until I told her. I had to go for some blood work a couple of years ago before you got out and she ended up being my lab tech. When she asked about you, I was really blunt. I told her you were in prison for killing her lover and she just passed out.

She was in the hospital for a couple of days and off work for over a week. I think even now she's still in a bit of shock. After she was released and went back to work, I looked her up and we went for coffee. I gave her an abridged version of what had happened. She didn't know. She'd left the college at the Christmas break and never heard about it at all."

"You mean she didn't graduate?"

"No, not from there. I guess her parents were really pissed at her. They never heard about the incident, is it alright to call it that?" I nodded. "They never heard about it until the trial started. All they knew is that she had cheated on you. By then Lynsy was in BCIT. She had no social life, had a job, and finished a year early by studying through the summers.

They never told her, and she hasn't really talked to anyone who knew the two of you. She's a lab tech at Woolston Labs in Fairview. She's got an apartment over there as well. She couldn't stay living at her parents' place. She's been there almost five years now."

"So she's doing okay," I took a few moments to digest all this. I really hadn't heard much about her at all since I went to prison. Of course, that was the way I wanted it. "Mike, we have to get back to the shop. Our next door neighbours are redecorating and we've got the contract."

"Yeah, I've got to get back to work too. Let's go, Lunch is on me," I paid the bill and left a generous tip. Servers are generally overworked and underpaid. I found it paid off to be a good tipper.

I dropped Lori and Mandy off in front of their shop. There were two people, I'd say in their fifties, waiting for them. They smiled at the couple, and as Mandy went to greet them, Lori leaned into the truck and said, "Think about it, Mike. Please. I think it would do you both good to talk about it. Even if nothing else happens, it'll at least clear the air. Thanks for lunch." She closed the door and followed the others into the shop before I could answer.

Over the next few months, we got really busy. Sam was out on jobs more than he was in the shop. Sonia easily handled most of the front counter stuff. I mostly looked after our business clients, helped in the back, and worked the front counter when I had to. It was starting to look like we might have to hire more staff if it got much busier. We weren't complaining. Sam and Sonia started dating but didn't talk about it at all at work.

About this time, I was starting to consider some sort of share plan where everyone got their regular wages, then a share of the profits at year end. I talked to the Credit Union manager and he gave me some pointers. He also told me to get a good tax accountant and talk it over with them. He gave me a couple of names and I made some phone calls. They were busy, so it would be almost two weeks before I could get it started.

There was one afternoon when we all happened to be in the shop. Sam and Sonia were up front, as usual, I was buried under paperwork and our two techs were going non-stop with repairs. We had a policy of twenty-four hours turn around unless we had to order parts. Then the customer was advised of the delay. We had a good reputation for honesty and service, two qualities necessary for success.

My intercom buzzed. "Yes?"

"Mike, we need you up front for a sec," answered Sam.

"Can't you handle it, Sam?"

"Nope, this one needs you."

"Okay, give me a minute." I walked up to the front of the shop wondering what on earth could be so difficult that they'd need me. I walked up behind the front counter and stopped and stared.

Lynsy! What the hell is she doing here?

So this is what it was about. I just glared at Sam and Sonia and turned around and walked through the workshop and out the back door without saying a word to anyone, slamming the door on my way out. My mind was racing in five different directions. I didn't know where I was going, I was just going. I found myself in a small park a couple of blocks away from the downtown area. There were only a few ducks and a couple of Canada geese around, no people at all.

Lynsy just stood there inside the door, tears streaming down her face. She made no attempt to wipe them.

"He really does hate me, doesn't he?" she said.

Sonia thought for a minute then replied, "No, Lynsy, he doesn't hate you. As a matter of fact, I think he's still in love with you."

"Even after...?" Lynsy mumbled.

"Yes, even after all that's happened. He never blamed you for his being sent to prison. He was trying to take his own life and got stopped by his roommate. The thing with, what was his name? Todd?" Lynsy nodded. "The thing with Todd was just an unfortunate circumstance of him being in the wrong place at the wrong time. You were never considered part of it."

"Why won't he talk to me then," Lynsy sobbed. "I talked to Lori and Mandy and they thought it might be a good idea to come here since he's hardly ever at home. Why did he run?"

Sam spoke up, "Lynsy. He's still hurt and confused about his feelings for you, even after all this time. He's afraid of saying or doing something that will hurt you, or him. Remember, this is the first time he's seen you for years, and he's so far refused to talk to anyone about what happened. I know what went down because I was his cellmate for six years. He's the one who taught me about computers and my speciality, networking. He had never, ever said anything about Todd being your fault."

"You were in...?" Lynsy wasn't sure she heard right.

"Yes, we were in the same cell for six years. I served eight of a ten-year sentence for basically the same thing, manslaughter. Mike served his full seven years. He applied for early parole only once. They turned him down so he never bothered to apply again."

"God, I never knew. I knew he'd been in prison, but seven years?"

"Well, only six were in prison. He spent the first year in a mental hospital because of his attempted suicide and depression. I don't think that part is very far away or even well known. Even now, he still fights the demons, every day. I know he goes for counselling about once a month."

"Is there somewhere I can sit down? I don't know if I can handle this," sobbed Lynsy. Sonia led her back to the rudimentary break room that they all shared. If the techs thought it was unusual, they never let on. They may not have even noticed. Techs can be like that.

"Here, have some water. Mike wouldn't have gone far. Probably just to the park a few blocks away," Sonia said. "I'm pretty sure that he's just in shock from seeing you standing there. I have to admit that I didn't think that walking out the back door would be his reaction."

"You think...?" Lynsy was sort of wondering out loud.

"Should you go find him? What have you got to lose? Either that or wait here for him to come back, which he might not do today. Look, I don't know you, just that you and Mike have a history. He's a great guy. He's the only one that would give me and Sam a chance. The only one that would hire us. Whatever you do, don't hurt him worse than he already is. I have to get back to work. You're welcome to hang out here if you want. We don't close for another couple of hours."

Sonia left Lynsy sitting in the break room, contemplating her next move. She finished her glass of water, rinsed the glass and put it on the sideboard. She checked to see that all the obvious signs of her tears weren't showing on her face, got her purse and jacket, and quietly went out the back door of the shop.

She spotted the park entrance, just where Sonia had said. As she got closer, she could see a lone figure sitting on a bench facing a pond. A few ducks and geese floated around, but he didn't even seem aware of them. My mind was swirling. All the events of the past nine or so years came screaming through my head. God damn it, everything was going so well. I had almost gotten Lynsy out of my conscious, though never my sub-conscious, and thought I could move on. Now what? What do I say? What do I do? I just buried my head in my hands. I felt really confused. I didn't hear the quiet footsteps come up behind me.

After a few minutes, I sensed her behind me. She hadn't spoken, just stood there. I didn't look and didn't speak. Maybe she'd just go away. After a few minutes, Lynsy said, "You know Mike, I killed a man too. Actually, I think I killed two men."

"Yeah, you're all about killing people." The anger I felt was obvious in my voice. "Oh, I don't mean I physically did it but I might as well have pulled the trigger," Lynsy replied. "What I mean is that I killed the man I loved by cheating. If I hadn't done that, the other wouldn't have happened."

Lynsy was sobbing, but I never turned around to look at her. "You know that I do love you, I always have. We need to talk. I want to talk. I need to explain..."

"You need to explain what? That you were fucking that football player on the side? What needs explaining? You cheated and tore the guts and heart out of me and you think you can explain that?" The anger hurt, and betrayal spat the words out for me. "I loved you with all my being and got rewarded by that! And you need to explain. Go away. Fuck off and leave me alone. There's nothing to explain. You did what you did, and I did what I did. It's finished." I still didn't look at her, afraid what I might say or do if I faced her.

She dropped a card on the bench beside me. "Please call. Anytime. Mike, please. We, I mean I, need to talk about this. Maybe nothing will come of it but it will help me, us, heal. We both need to heal Mike." With that, she turned and walked slowly out of the park and back to her car parked in front of the computer shop, a small figure with the weight of the world on her shoulders. She got into her car, collapsed into the seat and bawled her eyes out.

She was still there when Sonia looked out a while later, a lost figure sitting and staring out the windshield of the car and seeing nothing. Sonia thought about going out to talk to Lynsy, but decided against it. Obviously, the talk, if they even had one, hadn't gone the way she and Sam had hoped.

When they locked the shop a couple of hours later, Lynsy was gone. Mike hadn't returned to the shop that afternoon. They went to his apartment. There was no answer to their knock on the door. His truck was in its stall, but that was normal. Mike usually walked to work. At the park? They agreed to walk the short distance to see if he was there. They had to make sure he was okay. He might be the boss, but he was their friend.

They found me sitting on the bench where I'd been when Lynsy talked to me. "Hey, man. You okay?" Sam asked. I just nodded, not saying anything. "Look, back at the shop. You know. Well, we didn't..."

"If I thought you two had set this up," I said quietly, "you might be looking for work. But I'm betting on Lori and Mandy."

"Mike," Sonia spoke, "we didn't even know who she was until she told us. Oh, we know about her, but have never even met her until today."

"Okay, I believe you. I'll be okay. You guys just go. I'll see you on Monday." They hesitated a moment, made as if to speak but didn't. They walked out of the park hand in hand leaving a forlorn figure sitting on the bench watching the ducks and geese without really seeing them.

I pulled out my Blackberry and made a call.

Two hours later, with an iced tea at hand, I was sitting in my therapists' office relating the events of the afternoon. The therapist thought for a few minutes then said, "What do you want to do about all this Mike? I mean really do." He emphasized the word. "You obviously still have feelings for her, even though you try to bury them in your work. How's that working for you?" I just shrugged my shoulders.

"Here's what I think. Set up a meeting. Set it up in a neutral setting like a park or somewhere public, but where you won't be interrupted. Tell her how you feel, tell her everything. But, and this is really important, you have to let her have her say as well. You might even let her go first, but tell her the ground rules. Neither of you can walk away until you're both finished talking."

He went on to discuss how he thought the meeting could be put together. Just as I was getting up to leave, somewhat relieved to have been able to talk this out, the therapist asked a parting question, "Mike, you say you don't blame her for what happened. Is that really true, or are you just being noble? It's important for you to know what you really, and I do mean really, feel about it. It's no good if your true feelings on the matter are buried."

"Okay, thanks Doc. That's something to think about. Can we set up an appointment for late next week? I want to tell you how it goes."

"Good idea. How about a week from now, same time?"

"Works for me," I said as I quietly closed the door behind and went home.

Chapter 8

I returned to my apartment, reflecting on the day. It was, to say the least, eye-opening. I hadn't realized how Lynsy felt and had tried to put the thought of her or what she might be thinking out of my mind. I resolved to call her tomorrow and set up a meeting. Tonight I just wanted to relax and not think of anything, anything at all. I was in bed and asleep by ten without even having dinner. My appetite had deserted me in the park.

Sam and Sonia walked back towards the apartment block. "Sam, you want to come over for dinner? I know the girls would love to see you again. I don't know what we're having, but I can get something together."

"Sounds good. But how about this? We swing by the Burger Baron and pick up some burgers and a couple of kids meals, my treat."

"Are you sure? I know the girls love those kids' meals they have. I haven't had one of their burgers for ages."

"Good, it's settled. Let's go up to my apartment so I can get cleaned up then we'll head over." They walked up the stairs to his apartment. "Sorry about the mess. Typical bachelor pad. I'll just be a minute then we can get going."

Sonia didn't think it was all that bad, just disorganized. Certainly not as bad as some she had seen. She sat at the kitchen table thinking about their relationship. On their first date, he had come over to her apartment to pick her up. The girls fell in love with this huge Teddy Bear at first sight, especially when he got down on the floor to play with them.

They had been out several times and Sonia was thinking about taking it to the next level. What she didn't know is that Sam was having those exact same thoughts as he got ready. Maybe they'd talk about it tonight after the girls had gone to bed.

After burgers and cokes, they relaxed in Sonia's living room. The girls wanted Sam to try the latest video games, which he let them win. Sonia just looked on and smiled at the three of them. Eight o'clock came around and it was time for the girls to go to bed. Sam grabbed each one around the waist and carried them screaming and giggling into their bedroom, with Sonia following right behind. He left the three of them there as Sonia got them into bed.

"Sam, can you come in? Megan and Misty want you to help tuck them in. They also want a story, but I said no." Sam went into the bedroom and found the two girls already in bed. "They just want you to kiss them good night," said Sonia. He went and kissed each girl on the forehead, said goodnight to them, and he and Sonia retreated to the living room. "Do you want something to drink? I mean other than coke? I've got some wine in the fridge, a nice merlot from the Okanagan."

"Okay, just a small glass. I really haven't done much drinking since..., well you know. Mike kind of got me hooked on iced tea," replied Sam. "With him, you'd think there was no other cold beverage on the planet." Sonia giggled as she poured two glasses of wine and returned to sit beside Sam on the couch. She handed one to Sam and raised her glass, "To friends."

He replied, "To friends," took a sip then placed his wine on the coffee table. He then took her glass from her and placed it beside his, leaned over and kissed her. She responded by pulling him closer and kissing harder. "Damn, you. What took you so long?" she asked when they broke to come up for air. "I didn't want to chase you away. We were friends and I didn't want to get in the way of that," Sam said. "I've wanted to do that for so long."

"Me too," she said, pulling him in for another long kiss. She took one hand and placed it on her breast. They made out like a couple of teenagers when she pulled away, stood up and took him by the hand. "Please, be gentle. It's been a long time since I was with anyone who I cared for," she said softly as she led him into her bedroom. "We have to be quiet because of the girls."

"Oh, baby. I've wanted you for so long." Sam kissed her and began unbuttoning her shirt. Later on, lying cuddled together in bed Sonia asked, "What now? Do you think we have a chance?"

"Baby, I've wanted you since the first time I laid eyes on you. And those two little imps. I just don't think I'm good enough for you or them. You know, with my past and all. You don't know the whole story, nobody around here does." Sonia leaned over and kissed him. "I know enough. You're the man I want, the man I need. The girls adore you, and so do I. I'm hoping we can become a real couple. Come on, get dressed and let's go finish our wine and talk."

She got out of bed and put on a robe. Sam did the bathroom thing, got dressed and walked out to find her in the living room sipping on her glass of merlot. "Baby, let me tell you what happened that got me sent to prison. After that, you might change your mind. I really, really hope you don't. Here's what happened..."

I woke up early Saturday morning. I must have been exhausted and slept for nearly twelve hours. It took a few moments before I began to remember the events of yesterday. Ten AM, maybe Lynsy is up. I found the card she had left me and punched the number into my cell phone. There was no answer, so I left her a message to call me on her answering machine and went to have a shower. I'd already put the coffee on. It would be ready when I finished my morning ablutions.

I had just poured my first coffee when the doorbell rang. I expected it to be one of my sisters, so just pushed the button to allow them into the building. To my utter surprise, Lynsy was standing there when I opened the door. "Uh, Lynsy. I just called you. What are you doing here?" She was standing there in the doorway, a small figure with a scared look on her face.

"Mike, forgive me. I got your address from Lori. After yesterday I had to tell you what I'm thinking, what I'm feeling. All I ask is that you hear me out then I'll go if you want. Please, please." She was almost begging, so unlike the Lynsy, I knew from years ago. Of course, I had wanted to meet with her after discussing things with my therapist, but this certainly wasn't what I had in mind. I invited her in.

"Would you like a coffee? I just made it" I said as I put my coffee on the kitchen table and gestured her to sit down.

"Um, okay. I guess I could use a coffee."

"Cream, one sugar. Right?" I asked.

"You remembered," replied Lynsy.

"You'd be surprised at what I remember," I said as I put the mug in front of her then sat down across the table. She was still as lovely as ever, but she had changed. There was no spark of life in her eyes, and she looked sort of flat, almost unemotional. "I just called you to set up a meet somewhere. I really didn't expect you to be here."

"I know. But yesterday, after...well, yesterday I called Lori and talked to her for about two hours. She gave me your address and here I am. Mike, I know I can't undo what was done, but I have to tell you my side. After that, I'll go."

"Go on," I replied, stone-faced. My guts were churning but I didn't want her to know that.

"This thing with Todd. He seduced me. I have no excuse for that. None whatsoever. I totally fucked up and I know that. Mike, with him it was just the sex. It was just raw sex. With you and me it was love. We never had sex, we made love. I was only with Todd four times, just four Monday mornings. You know, that after the first two times it almost seemed scripted. I don't know how you found out, but when I saw our picture with the black "X" through it, I knew that my life as I knew it was over, that I'd lost you. Then the next day when you ran away from me when I was trying to catch up to you...well, I..."

"And I wouldn't let you try and justify your actions," I couldn't keep the bitterness out of my voice. "I heard you telling him it was getting better every time meaning that wasn't the first. If it had been, I might have acted different, but it wasn't. As much as it tore my guts and heart out, I had to cut my losses. I couldn't live a lie pretending I didn't know. And now I hear you tell him he's getting better. What the hell was I SUPPOSED to think? You know, I still have that old cell phone. The video I took of you two, along with the pictures is the only thing on it. It's seared into my head, you telling him that you had never had it so good. It's all there! Want to see it?" I was really getting pissed at her, and at myself, for not being able to let her go.

"Please, just hear me out. After it all came out, all our old friends turned against me. Leah Brown really told me off, as did some of the others. I deserved it all. I basically became a hermit and finished the semester, then left the college. I didn't know about any of the rest of it until I met Lori in the lab. My Dad sent me to BCIT to finish my certification. I lived with my Aunt there. We talked about what I had done. She already knew. She'd talked to my Mom and your Mom. She never told me that you were in prison. Nobody did until Lori in the lab. We met again for coffee a couple of times and she told me the whole story. I still have trouble believing everything that I caused."

"Anyway, my Aunt told me that she had made the same mistake when she was young, and she's still alone to this day. The love of her life moved on when she moved in with this guy. It turned out to be a mistake, but for her, it was too late. He fell in love with someone else and has a great family. My Aunt is even friends now, but she realizes that's all it will ever be. She told me not to make the same mistake. Not to make the same mistake and lose the man I love. Mike, that man is you." With that, Lynsy got up from the table and started towards the door. Her coffee was untouched.

"Can I say something before you go?" I asked. She stopped, turned around and stood beside the table. I could tell that she was just on the brink of tears. It wouldn't take much for them to fall.

"You know, when I found out it just tore the guts out of me. I'd lost my whole world. I have never felt so angry and betrayed in my life. You did the worst thing possible that I can think of; you broke a trust. I buried myself in my school work, my job and my tutoring. Todd even called to set up his next tutoring session. I guess he figured out that wasn't going to happen when I just hung up on him. Anyway, I had it all worked out. My pain was going to end, and I wouldn't have to worry anymore. Well, you know the rest. If Ed hadn't come through the door when he did..."

"Despite all this, I never stopped loving you, never blamed you for what happened after. I'm the one who's supposed to be dead, not Todd. I thought you two were together. Nobody told me differently, and I didn't ask. Yes, our friends turned against you, but I just avoided them. There was just too much pain, too much history, and the wounds wouldn't heal. Yes, even after all this time I still love you. I absolutely hate your cheating, that is inexcusable."

I stopped and took a huge breath. "I don't know what's going to happen now but I told my therapist and my real friends that I'd let you have your say. I don't know if I can get past your cheating; you're breaking a trust."

"Mike, I don't know if I can ever regain your trust. I'd like for us to try and get together again, but I totally understand if you don't want to. I'm going now. You can think it over and call me, or not." Lynsy got up from the table and let herself out of the apartment before I could reply.

Damn, damn, damn. I didn't want her to go, but I couldn't wait until she was gone. My mind was whirling. My coffee got cold, I didn't even notice.

Chapter 9

Sunday I just relaxed, well, as much as I could. There was nothing of interest on the tube, and I found myself reading the same pages of my book over and over. Damn. Lynsy. I was feeling totally confused. I went for a walk over to the park and walked around watching the kids feeding the ducks, old folks and young couples walking hand in hand, young families playing in the playgrounds. Everyone having a really good day; I had never felt so alone.

Monday found me in the office early, hours before any of the others would show up. When in doubt and you can't sleep, there's always paperwork. I'd been there about two hours when Sonia came in. She wasn't her normal cheerful self as she came into my office and closed the door.

"Mike," she was almost sobbing. "I don't know how to tell you this. Me and Sam got together..."

"Did he hurt you, cause a problem?" I interjected.

"No, no. It's not Sam. We had a great time together. It was wonderful. He stayed over until last night. The girls think they love him. I'm sort of leaning that way too. Even with his past, well, he told me. That's not the problem. It's my brother, my lowlife brother. He came to see me after Sam left last night. He threatened my girls, his nieces." Sonia went on to relate how he was trying to blackmail her into getting the banking codes for the business so he could steal from the accounts online.

He'd been watching her and saw that she was the one who usually made the weekly deposits. He figured that by threatening her daughters, he could blackmail her into giving him the access codes to the business accounts. The last thing he expected was that she would come to me and lay it out and ask for help.

"Okay, I think I've got it. You're supposed to get the online banking codes from me, give them to him so he can slowly bleed the company bank accounts, right?" She nodded. "Okay, let's make sure that that is exactly what he gets, with a few little wrinkles thrown in. What I need you to do is don't say anything to anyone. I'll make a couple of phone calls, and see what we can set up. Just do your best to be natural, and whatever you do, don't mention this to Sam. At least not yet. We don't need him mad just yet. Maybe later, but not yet."

Sonia was visibly relieved. "You mean something can be done. I mean to end this for once and for all. I just know that if it happens once and works, he'll keep doing this. I need to protect my girls. I love working here, it's a great job and I don't want to lose that."

"Sonia, leave it with me," I said. "I'll make a couple of calls and hopefully have it all set up in a day or so. How are you supposed to get the codes to him?"

"He gave me a phone number."

"Okay, keep it for now. Now go to work and don't worry. This will end in our favour. Just let me make some arrangements." Sonia walked back to the front of the store as I picked up the phone. Fortunately, the credit union manager, Fred, was into work early and answered his personal line. I made an appointment to meet with him and one of his computer security people just after the branch opened. I then went online and got a printout of current monthly transactions and did some calculating. An idea was forming but I didn't know for sure if the Credit Union system could do what I was thinking. Their security people would know, and they'd have to set it up.

Just after ten, I walked into the Credit Union and up to the managers' office. His secretary told me to go right in since I was expected. "Mike, come in. Sit down. Would you like a coffee? My security rep will be here in about ten minutes." He arranged for his secretary to get a couple of coffees then asked me what he could do for me. I explained to him what Sonia had related to me, and what I was thinking on how to set up a sting.

Just after ten-fifteen, his secretary announced that the security person had arrived. When she walked into the office, I was shocked. "Leah...?"

"Mike? What are you doing here?"

"Mike, Leah," the manager asked, "do you two know each other."

Leah answered, "We were in the same computer program at the university. I think I was tops in class and Mike was a close second." She turned to me, "What on earth are you doing here? After that, well, that happened I totally lost track of you."

"Leah, it's good to see a friendly face. It's okay, Mr Masters knows about what happened. I finished my degree in prison, then moved here and set up shop. We've been doing fairly well for the last year or so."

"Look," she said, "we need to do lunch or something to catch up. But later. Mr Masters really didn't go into detail, just that you needed to meet with him and me." I again related the events of the morning then explained to her what I thought we could do to set up a sting that would nail the brother for once and all. Leah made some notes, checked a couple of things in her manual (on her company laptop).

"You sneaky bugger. You know, this will work. He'll never see it coming and he certainly won't see it going. This is going to be a hoot." Leah gave a fist pump then gave Fred and me a big smile. "Sure beats doing the old routine security stuff. What timeline do we have?"

"I'd like to get it all done as soon as possible so the interruption at the shop won't be too big," I replied. "What do you think about having it all over by Friday?"

"A little tight, but I think we can get it done. Here's what I need you to do right now..." She went on to explain about setting up a dummy account and making it look like the company's operating account. If all went well, it would only be in use for just over a week. We got the account set up, obtained the online access code and got started. I told Leah that I could do the day to day stuff from my office so it would look like a legitimate account. She agreed that that was probably the best way to do it.

It was time for me to get back to the shop. "Fred, thanks for everything. I'll treat you and your wife to dinner when all this is over. Leah, how can I thank you? I'd really like to catch up sometime when you're back in this area."

"Mike, I'd love to get caught up. As you can see, I'm married." She flashed a huge diamond alongside her wedding ring. "We have a couple of great kids. Mark, my husband, works for the government. All hush hush and all that. I'd like for him to meet you. Look, do you have time for a quick coffee? I'd like to ask you a bit about what happened. All I know is up to the trial."

"Why don't you walk back to the shop with me? There's a great coffee shop next door to it, and I get a discount," I said as I stood to leave the office. "Lead on," Leah said as she took my arm. "This should get a few tongues wagging." We got outside the Credit Union and started down the street towards my shop about four blocks away. "So, what happened? Last I heard you were in prison. I thought you were sentenced to about 10 years?"

"No, the crown wanted 10 but I ended up with 7. I served the full seven and was released. I've got about another two years left on parole. Long story short, after I got out I moved here, got some seed money that was still on deposit in the Credit Union, found a storefront and went into business. So far we're doing pretty well."

We talked some more over coffee then Leah had to go. "Mike, please keep in touch. Here's my card. My personal email and cell are on the back. I'm really glad to see you doing well. You were one of the good guys and didn't deserve all the shit that got dumped on you." She gave me a brief hug and was gone, walking back to the Credit Union.

The week dragged by. It's funny how time stands still when you want it to fly. Sonia made the bank deposit on Friday, as usual. She didn't mention if she had met with her brother, and I didn't ask. We'd know this weekend in any event.

Sammy Johnson was in heaven. His stupid sister had bought the line that it was a one-time thing. Now he had the banking codes, he could bleed the company. He figured he was smart; he'd do small amounts that would take some time to get noticed. It should be good for around a hundred grand, maybe even more. He wondered how many times he could go to the well before she got cold feet.

He fired up his laptop and logged on. He tried logging onto the bank site and was happy to see that the access codes worked. To him, it looked like the account was a normal operating account. There were a few transfers out that looked like bill payments, and of course the usual weekly deposits. He logged off the bank site and found some porn on one of his favourite sites. He leaned back into his recliner and lit a joint. Yup, it was a good day. Tomorrow would be better.

Later that evening he logged onto his computer and the bank site again. He'd just got back to his apartment after watching Sonia make her weekly deposit at the Credit Union. He couldn't see anything out of the ordinary, so he assumed that she had done as instructed and told no one. He'd stopped her and got the codes as she was returning to the store instead of her phoning like originally said. He got busy and set up a transfer of funds out of the Operating Account to his own account in another institution. Figuring he'd start small, he transferred just under ten thousand dollars so as not to trigger any reviews of transfers of large amounts.

He pressed the key, and confirmation of the transfer flashed on the screen. "Good, I'll do it again in a couple of hours," he thought to himself. It was time for a little celebration. He left the apartment and headed down to a bar down the street.

Meanwhile, the transfer from the dummy account had triggered an alarm, just as Leah had set up. The amount of the funds, the IP address of the computer being used, and the intended destination account were all duly logged. The duty security officer at the data centre phoned Leah,

"There was a transfer from the account. We just got it on tape."

"Good, keep monitoring. Maybe he'll do another one. I'll be in around mid-night to work on the rest of it," said Leah. That was the part of the job she didn't like, the calls at any hour that required her attention. "Can't complain," she thought to herself, "this is what I get paid for. Besides, this one is for a friend."

At 11:28 the phone rang again. Leah wasn't really expecting another call but was hoping. "Another one just went through and was logged. Same IP."

"Okay, I'll be there in about half an hour. Did you phone the commercial crime unit and let them know?" she said, as she started putting on her jacket. "Yeah, after the first one. I'll give them another call. See you in a bit."

Leah drove into the data centre, parked her Lexus in her reserved spot and let herself in using her key card. Almost the last time for this, too, she thought. They were upgrading security to have access controlled by a retinal scan. She got to her desk and logged onto her computer before letting the duty officer know she was here. "Anything more?" she asked.

"Nope, just the two. Identical except for the times. Commercial crime has been advised. They're tracing the IP as we speak. It kind of helps to know who they're looking for. Just a matter of confirming it with the internet provider. They'll call and confirm. Meanwhile, I guess we can play." The duty officer was almost rubbing his hands. This kind of stuff broke up the monotony.

"Yes, let's get going. You know where to send the funds to. Grab it all as one amount and route it through a couple of data centres before depositing it into the legitimate account. If he logs on again, it will show that the money has been transferred out, but not where it went. The commercial crime guys can check his computer to see if he tries to log on to his own bank and check his account. What I'd give to be a fly on the wall when he does that." Leah smiled to herself as they got to work. The movement of the funds through the various data centres would require her authorization, other than that the duty officer looked after the rest of it.

Twenty minutes later it was done. The funds had been routed through Vancouver, Toronto and Montreal data centres, then back to the Calgary Data Centre and into its proper account. She checked to see that the deposit had been made to the legitimate account belonging to Mike, then logged off her computer. She stopped to thank the duty officer and went home.

Saturday morning found Mike back at the shop. If all went as planned, Leah would phone him there. While waiting, he tackled the never-ending mountain of paperwork that is the bane of any small business. Just after ten, the phone rang.

"Hello, Mike here."

"Mike it's Leah. It all went great. Commercial crime just phoned to tell me he's in custody. Along with his laptop, they found a bunch of drugs that it looked like he planned on selling. He's been remanded in custody since he has quite a record. They haven't got everything off his computer yet but should have it shortly. Tell your staff they can relax now. We can finish cleaning it up on Monday."

"Leah, I can't thank you enough. I know Sonia is almost a basket case with worry, even though she knows that it's not her fault. I'll go now so I can give them the good news. I owe you dinner. Bring your hubby."

"Okay Mike, I'm happy it went as planned. I'll get back to you about dinner. Take care now." As soon as the line cleared, I began to punch in Sonia's cell number then stopped and decided to go over to her apartment instead. Good news should be shared face to face. If Sam was there, I could tell them both at the same time. Ten minutes later I pulled into the visitors' parking lot at her apartment complex. I smiled to myself when I saw that Sams' car was parked closest to the entrance. I pushed the buzzer and waited for the intercom. No-one answered, but the door clicked open. I walked up to the third floor and knocked on the apartment door.

Sonia answered. "Mike, oh my God. Tell me. What happened? Did it go as you hoped? Is it over?" she was almost babbling. "Sonia, Sonia. Let's get a coffee going and I'll tell you all about it. Is Sam up, he should hear this too?"

"He's playing with the girls. Help yourself to coffee and I'll go get him." She left the kitchen and heard her calling Sam in one of the back bedrooms. Shortly they both returned; anxious looks on their faces.

"Okay, Mike, spill it," demanded Sam.

"Give me a sec. Let's go sit at the table while I relate what we've done. Safe to say that Sammy won't be bothering you or the girls anytime soon. Along with his incriminating laptop, they found a bunch of drugs in his apartment. He's been remanded in custody 'til Monday. They don't expect he'll make bail." Sonia almost collapsed with relief, leaning heavily against Sam.

Sam asked, "Why didn't you tell me about this before. Sonia just gave me bits and pieces and she doesn't know the whole story. What, exactly, did you do?"

"Okay, Sonia told you what she had told me, right?" Sam nodded, so Mike continued, "We knew that he followed her to the Credit Union when she made the weekly deposit and saw her stop and give him the account info that we'd set up. We thought she was supposed to phone him but he was there just after she made the deposit. One of the security guys had her under surveillance as soon as she left the shop until she got back. They didn't bother following him since they knew where he was going."

"What Leah, the head of security for the Credit Union had basically set up was a double transfer. When Sammy, or anybody, moved the money from my, our, dummy account he thought it was going straight into his bank account, and on his computer, it would look like it. He moved money twice, the same amount each time. What happened is that instead of going into his account, it was routed through a couple of data centres and into our legitimate account with the Credit Union.

There is no way for him to access that account. If he tried to trace it, even if he could, he'd probably lose it in the data centre traffic. After the second transfer out, the security people locked the dummy so nothing further could be taken out of it, but he could check to see that the money had been removed, just as he expected."

"The commercial crime guys are checking his computer as we speak. Leah will call me on Monday and fill in the details. Until then, we can relax and enjoy the weekend. Questions?" Sam said, "Why didn't you tell me about all this. Sonia's been a nut case all week and wouldn't tell me why. I finally got it out of her about that lowlife brother, but she couldn't tell me much more."

"Sam, if you knew, what would you have done?" asked Mike. "We had to make it look as normal as possible around here for the sting to work. What we didn't need is a big black bull charging around madder than hell and not able to do anything about it. Sonia played her part perfectly. I'm sorry we couldn't tell you, but that was a decision made by the security people. All on a need to know basis."

Sonia finally spoke, "I don't know about you guys, but I've hardly been able to eat for a week. How about some bacon and eggs?" We nodded, almost as one so she went into the kitchen and got busy. "Sam, you two an item now?" I asked quietly. "I guess my "blessing" at work worked out for you two."

"Mike, man. I don't think I've ever been happier. Got a great, beautiful woman and two wonderful girls. I've got a great boss and a good job. Life has sure turned around. I'm lovin' it," Sam answered.

"You set a date yet?"

"Nope. Haven't officially asked her. We're going to see Trooper tonight, and I was thinking of asking her after the concert. We just have to find a babysitter for the girls."

"Why not bring them over and they can bunk at my place. I'll get a couple of kids' movies and some pizza and they can camp out in the living room for the night. Give you two some privacy."

"Are you sure? Do you think you really want to look after a couple of wild young women?"

"Sure, not a problem. It's not like they don't know me. They've been in the shop often enough."

"Sounds like a plan, I'll check with Sonia." Sam was gone for about two minutes and came back with a huge grin on his face. "Sonia thanks you from the bottom of her heart, and so do I. We'll bring the girls over before supper so they can have their pizza. They've got air mattresses and sleeping bags so they really can "camp" in the living room. Thanks, buddy, this is above and beyond."

"Happy to help. At least your life is on track. Mine not so much, and no, we're not talking about it. Don't want to ruin the moment."

"Ruin what moment?" asked Sonia as she came into the dining room with a platter of bacon, eggs and toast. "Just hang on, I'll get the plates. Sam, can you find the silverware, please?" She came back in a minute with plates warmed from the oven. "Dig in, guys. Mike, you didn't tell me; ruin what moment, how?"

"The moment is this little celebration of the successful sting. How to ruin it would be you two trying to talk about my love life or lack thereof."

"Okay," Sonia didn't sound too convinced but decided that she didn't want to press Mike about the subject.

Chapter 10

Later that afternoon Sonia and Sam dropped the girls off at my apartment. They were loaded down with sleeping bags, a small suitcase and some toys. I had already picked up a couple of movies and the pizza. All I had to do was pop it in the oven for about half an hour.

"Good grief, you guys, I thought it was overnight, not movin' in."

The girls giggled, excited about this "campout" at their Moms' bosses home. "Mom said we're supposed to behave," said Megan, the older of the two. "She said you would make us sleep on the roof where the bats and birds can attack us," she giggled. "I don't think that's true, but that's what Mom said."

"I'd never let you sleep on the roof," I teased. "I've got nothing against bats and birds and what you two would do to them if you were up there." The girls giggled then broke out laughing. The mood was set for the evening. It was sometime after ten when I finally got them to go to the bed set up in the computer room. It was darker than the living room and right across the hall from the bathroom. They thought it was way cool sleeping near a bunch of computers. Maybe Uncle Mike would let them play on one tomorrow.

Late the next morning, I was relaxing with a coffee while watching the news. The two girls had woken early and begged and pleaded to be allowed to play on a computer. I finally gave in after they had their breakfast. I could hear them in the computer room/office laughing and giggling and having lots of fun.

"This is Mike," I picked up the phone on the second ring.

"Mike, Sonia. How are the girls? Were they any trouble?"

"Nope, no trouble. They kept me up past my bedtime, but I didn't make them sleep on the roof," I laughed. "They're in destroying one of my old computers. How was Trooper? You two have a good night?"

"Mike, I don't think we'll ever be able to repay you. If you've got the coffee on we'll be right over to tell you all about it."

"I'll put on a fresh pot. Should be ready by the time you're here."

"See you in a bit."

About fifteen minutes later the buzzer sounded their arrival, even though Sam could have just opened the door. Maybe they wanted to give me a heads up. I propped the door to the apartment open and just left it for them to find their own way in. It's not as if they didn't know the way by now.

Sonia had that special glow of a woman totally in love; Sam just looked tired, but couldn't stop smiling. "Man, I hope that coffee is ready," he said. "It was quite a night, and we were both totally sober." I laughed and told them to grab a seat in the living room. I went and told the girls that their mom was here, then went to get the coffees. As I handed coffee to Sonia, I could see a good size engagement ring on her finger. "Computers are more important," she grinned, explaining why the girls weren't around. "You see that he finally popped the question last night. Were you in on it?"

"No, not really. All I agreed to do was babysit so you two would have an evening alone. Congratulations, really. I hope you two will be totally happy ever after. Have you set a date yet, or is that too early?"

"No, but we're thinking of around Thanksgiving. That way we'll be married and have the honeymoon over with before the Christmas season starts. You remember what last year was like, totally crazy."

And so it was settled. The wedding would take place in early October with a honeymoon following. Sonia and Sam didn't want a large wedding, just a few friends and whatever family could arrange to get time off to make the trip. Sonia enlisted the help of a couple of her girlfriends to start making the necessary arrangements. They would also be the bridesmaids while their husbands would be the ushers.

Sam had asked me to be his best man and of course, I agreed. I designed the invitations and made a few phone calls that Sam and Sonia weren't aware of. Their little wedding would be somewhat larger than they expected. They didn't know just how many clients also considered them to be friends.

Over the next few months, we were really busy. I'd scored a couple of new corporate accounts which kept Sam and me busy. The walk-in traffic was steady enough that the two techs I'd hired were almost routinely working overtime. The business had become more successful than my wildest dreams, and in a far shorter time than I ever expected. We were quickly outgrowing our small store, and I began to search for a new location.

I mentioned this to Mary, of course, and she made a different proposal than our shop simply moving to another location. I still had the first option to buy the whole building, so why not convert the coffee shop into an internet cafe. Properly designed, we'd have the extra room to work that we needed. Mary and I sat down and began to put a plan together. Since she wanted to ease into retirement, she'd be happy to run the cafe part of the business, but would want someone to help out and gradually take it over.

I talked to Fred at the Credit Union, and he could see no problem if we needed financing. Now it was a matter of finalizing the plan and finding a contractor who could do the job the way we wanted it done. Mary was a goldmine of information and had numerous contacts in the business community. She finally decided to get together with an older gentleman and his son who had a good reputation.

It kind of helped that she had known the family for years. We told him what we wanted to be done and how we wanted it done. He made a few notes and a couple of suggestions that were incorporated into the plan, then left, saying that he'd have a price for us in about two days. He returned a couple of times to get some more information and take some photos and make more notes. He didn't tell us what he was doing; just that it had something to do with the quote he was preparing.

I went back to work, diving into the growing pile of paperwork that had to be done. The concept of the internet cafe was exciting since I knew of several in other towns that had become very successful. Once we got it going, it would be a matter of finding the right people to staff it. And I had nearly forgotten that I'd be losing Sam and Sonia for about two weeks. I'd have to find a way to work around them being gone as well. It was then that I considered maybe shutting down the store for a two week period while they were on their honeymoon. If we planned it right, and the contractor was willing, we could have the expansion done and the internet cafe in operation by the time they got back. I went to talk to Mary.

Two days later Mary called me and said that Max and his son were in the coffee shop with the proposal. I let Sonia know I was going next door but I wasn't sure for how long. She promised to hold down the fort.

Max had a bunch of papers spread out over one of Mary's largest tables. He had made some sketches of what he thought we wanted and what would work. Over the next couple of hours, we discussed the different aspects and finally came to an agreement. The cost to us was less than I expected, so financing wouldn't be a problem. Max said he would have an engineer draw up some blueprints and his son would do some concept drawings to show what the building would look like after they were done.

The blueprints were more for the government so we could get the permit. Max promised to look after that as well since he was more used to dealing with the bureaucrats than either me or Mary. He also agreed that closing the shop for two weeks would be a wise move and allow him and his men to work without interruption. Max said that he would have his lawyer draw up a formal contract and have it delivered to us, or to our lawyer, to review. This should take about a week since it was a fairly standard job.

A week later, Mary's lawyer called and said that the contract had been delivered and he was going over it. We made an appointment to see him the next day which would give him time to go over it and make sure there were no surprises. We weren't expecting any problems, but it paid to be certain.

We met with the lawyer the next afternoon. He said that it was a fairly standard contract and there were no hidden surprises. He went through it with us then we signed it. The original would go back to Maxes lawyer, we were given copies. I made an appointment with the Credit Union to arrange bridge financing, and we were on the way. Construction would start the day of Sam and Sonia's wedding.

Chapter 11

It was a beautiful, cool, crisp October afternoon when Sam and Sonia were married in a civil ceremony held in the community park. Much to their amazement, there were nearly two hundred people there due to some of the phone calls I'd made. Sonia's daughters were the flower girls and they giggled their way down to the front of the gathering, spreading flower petals all over the ground, guests seated near the aisle, and themselves. They were having a blast.

Sam and I stood in front of the Dias and watched, as the organ began the wedding march, as a vision of stunning beauty walked towards us escorted by a long time friend of her family. Sam was having trouble breathing, and I felt much the same. As she arrived, I stepped back and the ceremony began. It was over almost before we knew it since there were no sermons to sit through, just two people very much in love saying their vows.

After the ceremony, Sam, Sonia, the bridesmaids, flower girls, ushers and I left with the photographer while all the guests headed to the community hall just across the park from where the ceremony had been held. Sam and Sonia hadn't wanted a fancy meal, just a good old-fashioned smorgasbord and an open bar. Of course soft drinks, coffee and tea were also available since there were quite a few kids running around. They'd hired a DJ for music and dancing later.

Photographs finished, we headed into the hall to be met by all the guests. We mingled, got some beverages and then began the reception. Of course, the normal toasts to the bride, groom, their families, etc. were made, as well as some hilarious speeches by people who had worked with Sam or Sonia or had been involved somehow in business dealings with them. I'd arranged with the master of ceremonies to be the last speaker. Sam and Sonia had no idea that I was going to speak outside my duty toast to the bride.

"Sam, Sonia. I can't begin to tell you how much this day means to me. Yes, it's your day, and that's the way it should be. But, I like to think that somehow I had a small part in making this happy day happen, and that's why I find it so special. When you both approached me, at different times of course, about the "no dating" policy that I had, and after I had explained that it applies to only me, not the staff, I had no way of knowing that this would be the result. I think I speak for everyone here that we're all mighty glad that Sam saw the light once I explained the facts of life to him."

I paused and looked around. "Sam, since that very unhappy day a few years ago when we met, you've become my best friend and confident. I know, and you know, that things could have turned out a lot more different than they did. I say unhappy because of the circumstances under which we met, not the fact that we did meet. In retrospect, I think it's one of the best things to ever happened to me. That being said, there is no way that I can continue to have you and Sonia as employees."

You could have heard a pin drop. Shocked faces looked my way as I tried, somewhat successfully I hoped, to keep a serious face. "No, no longer will you be employed by me because I have here in my pocket documents drawn up by my lawyer that make you, as a couple, full and equal partners in our business. That is my wedding gift to two of the nicest people I've ever had the pleasure of meeting."

The roar that followed almost blew the walls out of the building, and Sam almost smothered me as he pounded my back and hugged me. Tears were freely flowing from Sonia, my sisters, and most of the people there. It took a long time for things to settle down.

Once things quieted down somewhat, the master of ceremonies looked over at me and asked, "Mike, is there anything else you'd like to add. It would really be hard for you to top that one."

"Just one thing. Let's get this party going." And we did into the early morning hours. I wasn't quite sure when Sam and Sonia had managed to leave. The girls were going to be looked after by their grandmother at Sonia's apartment until the honeymooners got back. I only had a couple of glasses of wine with dinner so I was in pretty good shape to do some taxi driving if need be, but it never turned out that way. Almost everyone had come to enjoy a good party, not get loud and drunk.

Next day I went to the shop to find Max, his son, and their crew hard at work tearing apart the coffee shop since that is where most of the changes would be made. I left them to it, promising to stay out of the way, and went into my office to tackle the ever-present paperwork. Having the shop closed except for emergencies freed up lots of time for me to get caught up. If any of our business customers needed some support, I'd handle it or get one of the techs to go over and check it out. Max had promised to hire both of them to help with the construction, using their technical skills to run wire and set up the wireless hotspots. At least they would be getting paid for their work, and they'd get some networking experience under their belt.

Over the next week, Mary popped in to check on how things were going every day or so. We'd chat a bit and end up going up the street to another cafe for lunch. She was really excited to see what was happening and really looking forward to seeing the finished product; as was I.

It was the Friday after we'd sat down for our usual lunch, when Mary said, "Mike, I think I understand where you're coming from with your old flame, Lynsy. I don't know if you're aware than Lori and Mandy, and even Sonia, and I have talked about her various times. I think even Debra has mentioned it a few times when she came in for coffee. I know the whole sordid story, how she wronged you. As a friend, can I give you some advice?"

I was silent for a minute, toying with the food on the plate that I no longer wanted. "Just what did you have in mind?" I asked quietly. "Just this. You either have to let her go and get on with your life or alternatively, work on getting her back and letting her gain your trust. You can't go on as you are with this eating at you like some damn cancer. It's not good for her, and it's really not good for you. You've got a real chance to build a good life here, but you have to let yourself live to do it. I don't have the answers; I'm not God, just a friend. Only you know, only you can figure out what you should do. Nobody else can do that. I just know that you had better do it soon because I can see the whole thing eating away at you. I'll help all I can, but in the end, it's up to you."

I sat there without answering. I knew she was right, but I really didn't have any idea which way I wanted to lean. Would I ever be able to trust Lynsy again or would that doubt always be there, hanging like the Sword of Damocles over our relationship? Would she, would I, ever be able to put that away and have a normal, loving partnership? I'd been badly burned once, should I take a chance again? And Lynsy, could she ever forgive me for the way I treated her? Yes, she had wronged me, but she didn't deserve the hell she'd gone through. Of course, much of that I had no control over, or knowledge of, but still...

"Mike, Mike," Mary's voice brought me back to the present. "I thought I'd lost you there for a minute."

"I was just letting the various options go racing through my head. Nobody was winning, yet."

"It will be tough, I know, but this is the perfect time to work it out. It's relatively quiet and you have another week before Sam and Sonia get back and the cafe and store reopen. If it will help, I'll get together with both of you and go from there."

"Thanks, Mary. You're a good friend, but this is something I, we, I mean me and Lynsy have to work out. Maybe I'll take the rest of the day off to think about it and give her a call."

"Sounds like a good idea. If you need a sounding board, you have my number. By the way, you're buying the lunch you didn't eat," she laughed. I hadn't even noticed that I'd hardly touched my plate. I was able to smile at her, then went and paid for our lunch, leaving a generous tip.

We left the cafe and separated, Mary to her home, me to take a walk in the park. The autumn air was crisp with a definite bite to it. Winter was well on its way. I let the phone ring four times, on the fifth ring I got the answering machine. "Lynsy, Mike. I'm just wondering if you'd like to get together for coffee or something. Please call me back and let me know. Bye for now."

Well, now the ball was in her court. Maybe she was at work or something. I turned on the tube and tried to find something worth watching. It was dark when the strident ring of the phone woke me up.

"Uh, Mike here. Hello," I mumbled.

"Mike, it's Lynsy. Did I wake you?"

"Uh, yeah. I must have fallen asleep watching the tube."

"When do you want to go for coffee? Where? I'm so glad you called. I was at work."

"Actually, I'm fairly flexible for the next week, so you name the time. I know you work, but I don't know your schedule, of course."

"I work most days, and have every third weekend on call. How about tomorrow early afternoon since I'm off this weekend?"

"How about we maybe do lunch? Does that work for you?" What the hell, I had to eat sometime didn't I?

"Sounds great. How about you pick me up and we'll decide where to go from there? You know where I live don't you?"

"Uh, no. Just your phone number."

"Okay. I'm in the Fairfax Apartments in Fairview. It's on 12th, about two blocks from the hospital. Apartment 201."

"Okay, how about I get there for noon?"

"Oh Mike, you don't know how much this means to me. I'll see you tomorrow." She disconnected, and I got up from the sofa and fixed something to eat. I didn't sleep much that night, at once dreading and looking forward to the next day.

Chapter 12

"Hey Tim, I know it's Saturday but can I talk to you for a few?" I asked my parole officer. "It's not about parole or anything, but I need an objective opinion."

"Hi Mike, when's good for you. I'm pretty much open. Not much happenin' here at home right now."

"Uh, well. Tim, it's a personal thing so I don't think your office is the best use for this. Could we just meet for coffee or something?"

"Okay Mike, I understand. How about we meet at the Coffee Coral? Say an hour? You're buying."

"Sounds good, thanks, Tim."

I pulled into the parking lot of the Coffee Coral just as Tim was going through the door. I threw my truck into park and followed him inside. He was just heading to a booth near the back. Good. We wouldn't be interrupted.

The server took our orders and we chatted about nothing in particular until the coffees arrived. "Okay Mike," Tim said as he spooned sugar into his coffee, "what did you need to talk to me about?"

"Well, it's not you, in particular, Tim, but I need someone who can give me an honest, objective opinion about something."

"Well, I can probably do that, but it would help if I knew what you're talking about," he grinned at me, trying to lighten the mood. "Well, you remember with all that had happened, there was a girl, woman, involved, right?"

"Yes, Alice or something like that if memory serves."

"Her name is Lynsy. Anyway, I'll give you a brief recap just to refresh your memory..." I went on to relate the events before and after the shooting. Most of these Tim was aware of since he was still my parole officer."... and so, I'm hoping you can give me an idea of how I should handle this. Should I really try to get together with her, or just let her go. I know she screwed up, but I'm no saint either and don't pretend to be. But I never, ever cheated on her. Not once, and not even since getting out of prison. I've just been too busy for a social life."

"Okay, Mike, so what you're saying is that you sort of want to get back together with her but you're afraid of getting hurt again, right?" I nodded. "Okay, it seems to me that you have to ask yourself a couple of questions and then honestly answer them, or get honest answers to them."

"Okay."

"First, do you really think that she had planned to leave you when this all started? You say she was chased by this Todd until she finally gave in. You said she indicated that she broke it off, but was she going to before she got caught? Second, she broke a trust once, but only once by her own admission. Everyone screws up, you just happened to be in the way of this one. Has she been dating anyone since you caught her?"

"No, I don't think so. She sees my sister Lori quite often for coffee and Lori has never mentioned anyone. All she says is that Lynsy is always asking about me."

"Okay, fair enough. She's been sort of faithful, at least to a memory. Now a big one. How well do you really know her? People change, and there's been a lot going on that affected both of you over the past few years, you especially. It's been nearly ten years since this all started and yet neither one of you seems to want to move on. Do you really believe she wants to resume your relationship since she probably doesn't know you that well either? Maybe she's just holding on to what used to be."

"I think you just hit the nail on the head. Do I really know her, or am I like you're thinking? Am I willing to get together with the current Lynsy, or just the Lynsy I knew years ago? To tell the truth, I really don't know her anymore, and she probably doesn't know me that well either."

"Well, try this. Tell her that. Be honest up front. It could be that she never thought of that part either. Then, if everything is okay from that point, start off as if it were a brand new relationship. The worst that could happen is that you go your separate ways. The best, well, that would be up to you two, wouldn't it?"

"Tim, I can't tell you how much I appreciate your insight. Every time I start thinking about this my mind goes in ten different directions all at once. Now, how are Lori and Mandy doing? I haven't seen them for a couple of weeks. They missed the family Lorieque a couple of weeks ago, and I couldn't make it last week." I relaxed back in my chair, feeling better than I had for quite some time.

"They're doing good. They got that contract for their neighbours' place and it sort of snowballed from there. They might even hire my wife, Meg, to handle the phone and stuff. At least it would get her out of the house once in a while."

We chatted for a while longer then left the restaurant. Of course, I picked up the tab. I jumped into my truck and waved to Tim as I exited the parking lot and headed back to Kent. He had certainly given me something to think about, and some questions to ask Lynsy. I decided that what future we had would be determined by her answers. I'm sure she had questions for me too, but I had no idea what they might be. She'd been getting info on me from Lori and Mandy for months, years.

Next morning I was up fairly early for a weekend. I was on the road to Fairview by 10:00 AM since I wasn't sure where her apartment was. Turns out it was easy to find, and I was outside the door of the Fairfax Apartments just before 11:00. I locked up the truck and went to push the call button.

Lynsy must have been watching for me because her metallic voice came over the intercom telling me to come up at the same time the door clicked open just as I pressed the buzzer. Apartment 201 was easy to find. It was in front of the building, down at the end of the hall opposite the elevator and stairs. I had taken the stairs.

Lynsy was waiting in the doorway as I walked down the hall to her apartment. She looked lovely standing there in the ambient light, dressed very conservatively as if going to church. She had, in fact, just returned from there. "Mike, come in. I just have to change out of my church going clothes and we can go. Would you like some coffee, I just put some on?" Her tone was sort of friendly neutral as if she was uncertain about what might happen. I felt the same way. I had no idea how this day might go.

"Sure, coffee sounds good. I'm way early so we have lots of time."

"No problem. Go have a seat in the living room. I'll get your coffee. Black, right?"

"Yes, please," I answered as I sat down in one of the large armchairs. There was another matching chair against another wall and a matching love seat in front of the French doors. I looked around as she handed me the coffee. The apartment was clean and neat as a pin, a far cry from mine. I wondered if this was normal, or if she had cleaned up to make an impression. I guess that was unfair, but I did wonder about it.

Lynsy walked up the hall to her bedroom. I could hear the rustling of clothes since she didn't close the door. In a few minutes, she came back into the living room dressed in casual slacks and a sweatshirt. There was some kind of logo on it, but I couldn't make it out. She went and got a coffee then sat down in the other armchair.

"Mike, I told you that you have no idea how much this means to me, and I meant it. I've been hoping, praying for this day for a long, long time." She leaned back in her chair trying to look casual, but her body language screamed tense.

"Yeah, you did say that. I've wanted to call but kept putting it off. I've really been torn about what to say, what to do. Lynsy, I'm not sure what's going to happen, or if we'll even have a relationship, but I do need to ask you some questions. Stuff that's been bugging me for years."

"Go ahead," she said quietly.

I took a couple of deep breaths then said, "You told Lori and Mandy that the day I found out about you and Todd; that you were going to break it off with him. Is that true? Were you really going to stay with me or leave me for a better fuck?"

Her face reflected the bluntness of the question. I'm not a politician, so I usually say exactly what I'm thinking. Sometimes it gets me into trouble, but over the years I've found it works best for me.

"Well, that's putting it out there, isn't it?" she replied, not angry or upset, sort of neutral. "Yes, I was going to break it off with Todd. I was going to tell him that night that it was all over. I had planned on staying with you, forever, since all he was, was a fuck, as you put it. I told you before he was just that, a fuck. You and me, we, made love. There's a huge difference. The worst part about it is my being unfaithful to you, that is unforgivable.

I still haven't forgiven myself, so I can't expect that you would either. Was it exciting with Todd? I'd be dishonest if I said no, but after the first couple of times it was pretty routine; almost like it was scripted. There was no love, no intimacy. I think I was just another notch on his prick."

"Okay, fair enough. I think you sort of said that before, but I had to know." I paused for a minute then asked," Lynsy, do you really know who I am? Do you want a relationship with me, or with the me that used to be? I'm not that person, Lynsy, and never will be again. There's been far too much happen." I was still speaking quietly, in a neutral tone. I wasn't either hopeful or discouraged, I just didn't know at this point.

She thought about that for a few minutes. "Mike, believe it or not until Lori told me you were in prison I had no idea of what happened. I was in love with the you that you used to be, and heartbroken when you wouldn't even talk to me after, well, after you caught us. Over the past few years, I've got together with Lori and Mandy for coffee fairly regularly. Lori told me how you had changed, some for the better, some not. She told me how when you got out of prison you went into business, and how successful you're becoming.

What really surprised me though, was that there was no indication that you were bitter, or blaming others, me, for what happened. You had taken responsibility for what you did and didn't blame circumstances, or finding me with Todd, or anything like that. You did it, you admitted to it, and served time for it, and in a lot of ways came out of prison a better man than you were before. There are not too many people that could ever say that, and you're the only one I've ever heard people say that about."

She stopped for a couple of seconds and took a huge breath, "So I guess the short answer is that, no, I don't know the Mike Foster that exists today, although I know a lot about him from others. Am I in love with the used to be Mike? No, I don't think so. He and the old Lynsy used to exist in another time, a time when we were carefree and had our whole lives ahead of us. I love the memories of that time. As for the new Mike, it's too early to tell. I don't know if he wants to know me, or even have anything to do with me."

I sipped at my almost cold coffee before replying, "Wow, that's a lot to take in all at once. Lori and Mandy did try to talk to me about you several times, but I made it plain that it was a taboo subject. She did tell me about your life and what happened to you after, well, after all that. My guess is that it hasn't been all that easy for you. Do you have any social life, no boyfriends, girlfriends?"

"After all that happened, I decided that I wasn't going to get hurt again and I wasn't going to hurt anybody again either. So I've basically become a sort of recluse. I work, I go for walks, I read, sleep and eat. That's about it. I really don't have or want, any close friends. I do go out with the girls from the lab for a drink once in a while, but not too much. You know I meet Lori and Mandy for coffee and there are a few others. I'm single and alone, not lonely. I can't say I'm happy with my life, but I'm fairly content. Oh, I've been asked out lots of times, but only went on a few dates. They were nice enough, but there was no spark, no feeling of wanting to build a relationship."

"Sounds almost like me, except I do get to the family Lorieques on Saturdays. Other than that, it's just work, no play." She got up to refill the coffee's as I continued, "You know, much like you, I decided that I never want to be hurt like that again, and for me, the best way to make sure of that is to not put myself in a position where it could happen. You know, of course, that my roommate caught me with a shotgun in my mouth. He got it away from me before I could pull the triggers. The hurt, the pain, the betrayal was so bad I just wanted to get away from it all. There's the odd day once in a while where I still feel like that. It's a good thing my therapist is on speed dial."

"Lori did mention the suicide attempt. It just tore me up, what I had done, what I had caused. That's one of the reasons I was hoping you would call, so somehow I could make that up to you. I don't know if you'll ever be able to forgive me for that." She was quietly sobbing now.

"There's nothing to forgive. I don't, and didn't, blame you for any of it. Oh, I did at the very first then I started to think there was something wrong with me that you'd hook up with, well, someone else. It took me a long time to come to terms with how I dealt with what happened. Until my sentencing, I didn't really know what depression was. With the hospitalization for a year and monthly therapy since I got out, I think I could write a book on it now, at least on how it affects me and how I deal with it."

I was still speaking quietly, intently, trying to impress on her just what I was trying to say, what I was feeling. I don't know if I was succeeding or not. My problem was, I didn't really know if at all what I was saying was the truth, or just that I'd been stating it for so long it sounded like the truth. Did I, or didn't I, deep down blame her for everything, and I just won't admit it? My therapist and I had knocked this around quite a bit and had never come to a firm resolution.

Tears were running down her face. She made no attempt to wipe them away. "You have every right to blame me, put the blame where it really belongs."

"You're right, I could. But would it solve anything, would it undo the past, would it help either of us in the future? I don't think so. It happened, and it's over. That's the way I look at it now." I took a deep breath and decided to go for it. "Lynsy, I love the thought of being in love with you again. Will it happen? I don't know, but I'd like for us to try."

"Oh my God, Mike. You don't know how much I've wanted to hear those words. It's something I've hoped and prayed for, for years." She was openly sobbing now but in relief. It took a few minutes for her to regain her composure. "I know we're supposed to go out for lunch, but I don't think I can. Not now. Why don't I throw something together and we can stay here and visit? There's so much I want to tell you, so much I want to ask."

"I think that's a plan. I don't much feel like putting on my public face right now. What can I do to help?" I was sort of relieved. I didn't really want to leave the comfort of her apartment. It was time to learn about each other and see if there would, could, be any kind of a relationship.

Together we made a couple of sandwiches, got some fresh veggies and homemade cookies and had lunch.

Lynsy put on a fresh pot of coffee. We sat at her kitchen table, almost like old times, and chatted the whole afternoon away. I learned about how her parents had heard about her cheating and our breaking up, how she was made to confront my mother and sisters, her life in Burnaby while at BCIT.

She hadn't had an easy time of it, but neither had I. I told her about prison and getting my degree there, the classes I had taught, my fathers' funeral. She admitted that she hadn't gone, knowing she wouldn't be welcome. I guess it wasn't her I'd seen at the burial.

It was late afternoon when I finally decided I had to leave. There was a lot we had discussed that I had to take in. Lynsy walked me to the front door of her apartment block. "Mike, oh Mike. I'm so glad you made that call. I've really enjoyed this afternoon, well, most of it anyway. Do you have any inkling of what might happen to us?"

"Lynsy, I'm glad too. What's going to happen? I don't know, but I know I want to see you again, take you out for a good dinner, have a real date."

"I'd love to do that, too. Just tell me when."

"I'll have to check my day book. I don't think I have too much scheduled for the next week. We're doing renovations so the shop is closed but I might have to look after some of our corporate customers. Can I call you?"

"Please, anytime. If I'm not here call my cell or leave a message." She gave me a quick kiss on the lips and returned to her apartment. I walked to my truck, deep in thought. Oh well, in for a penny, in for a pound. Maybe it will work out. Time will tell.

I was busy the next week. With Sam and Sonia on their honeymoon, I got to respond to all the calls that Sam would normally take. I was quite happy to do that since it gave me a reason to re-connect with our customers. The renovations were coming along with Maria supervising the crew re-doing the restaurant part.

We still hadn't found anyone to help her, but I didn't expect to start searching in earnest until after we re-opened. I was able to catch up on the never-ending paperwork as well as taking care of our customers. I was starting to appreciate just how much work Sam had been doing. It was a good move, making him and Sonia full partners.

On Wednesday I called Debra, "Deb, still doing the yard clean-up and Loriie on Saturday?"

"Yeah, Mike. Bring your work gloves and be prepared to get dirty."

"Can I bring a guest? I'm sure they'll pitch in to help."

"Of course. Anyone, we know?"

"Well, Sam and Sonia aren't due back till late afternoon so I doubt it, but you'll see. See you on Saturday. 'Bye Sis."

"Bye Mike, see you Saturday."

I called Lynsy, but her phone went to the answering machine. Of course, she's working. I didn't want to call her cell if she was working so I left a message for her to call me. At least at the family Lorieque, it would be neutral territory, sort of, and she would know almost everyone there.

Lynsy called me back later that evening. I told her that she should wear grubbies since we'd have to work for our supper, but I didn't tell her where we were going.

Saturday morning I got my stuff together and headed to Fairview. I had told Lynsy I'd pick her up before noon so we could grab a bite to eat on the way. We didn't have to be at my sisters' place at any set time, but I wanted to get there fairly early in the afternoon. There was work to do. We grabbed a quick sandwich and coffee at the Coffee Coral and headed to Bridgeville. I still hadn't told her where we were going, but she was okay with that. At least we were together.

I pulled up in front of Debra's home. "Okay, we've arrived. Here are some gloves. You might need them."

"Uh, okay Mike. Just where are we anyway?"

"My sister Debra and her hubby live here. You'll like Gerry, he's a great guy."

"Are you sure about this? I mean, the last time I saw Debra I wasn't in her good books."

"Just go with it. I asked to bring someone with me but didn't tell her it was you. Lori and Mandy will be here too, and Jimmy might even bring his latest flame."

She sounded sceptical, "Well, okay. If they don't mind..."

"Relax. They'll be happy to see you. Water under the bridge and all that. And anyway, you see Lori and Mandy all the time."

We walked around the house and into the backyard. Debra started, "Mike, 'bout time," then noticed who was with me. "Lynsy," she shrieked, "It's Lynsy. My God, how are you?" She came running over and enveloped Lynsy in a huge hug. "Mike said he was bringing someone, but he never said it was you. Come, come. Sit down. Can I get you something? Are you two...?"

"Sis, give it a rest. She's my date for the family Lorieque. I told her that you would be a slave driver and make her work for her supper." I was smiling at her reaction. Debra came over and gave me a hug, "I'm so glad to see you together. Lori and Mandy will be thrilled. Jimmy too, if he comes."

Debra introduced Lynsy and Gerry, who remarked that he was happy to meet the mystery woman he'd heard about. Debra got some coffees for her and Lynsy and made it known that Gerry and I were on our own as far as yard work goes. She and Lynsy had some catching up to do.

Lori and Mandy showed up a bit later and resulted in the same shrieking and hugging. Of course, Lori and Mandy had been meeting Lynsy off and on for quite a while, so there was no catching up on their part. Still, they were happy to sit and chat while Gerry and I worked. It wasn't onerous, and I enjoyed being out in the fresh air away from my desk.

Jimmy and his girlfriend, Jane, showed up a bit later. She was a cute little blonde with a bubbly personality. She and Jimmy seemed to get along great. I later learned they'd been together about four months and were officially a couple. Jimmy came down to the back of the yard where Gerry and I were working. We continued cleaning up the yard and talking. The women sat at the picnic table chatting and having coffee. We bitched and moaned until Debra and Lynsy took pity on us and brought us some coffee as well. Lynsy handed me mine then sat on the ground beside me to finish hers while I drank mine. I could see that some of the sparks were back in her eyes. This family outing had been a good move.

Coffee break over, Gerry, Jimmy and I got back to work. Gerry had one huge, old pine tree in his yard as well as several smaller trees. The pine had some dead branches just out of reach from the ground. We decided that they should be removed since we were doing the whole yard. I'd always climbed trees and almost anything else when I was a kid, so I told Gerry to forget about the ladder. Just hand me the saw after I climbed up.

"You sure, Mike? It's no big deal to get the ladder," Gerry asked.

"Hey, I haven't climbed a tree for years, but it's like riding a bike. Some things you don't forget," was my cocky reply. I handed him the pruning saw and I began climbing up the tree. I really didn't have to go too high, maybe ten feet or so. Gerry handed me the pruning saw and I began to cut the dead branches, allowing them to fall to the ground. All was going well until I was holding onto one branch and cutting another when the branch I was holding onto broke. The last thing I remember was hearing the sickening crack as my left leg broke, just above my ankle. The fall knocked me out.

Chapter 13

I came to in the hospital. At first, I didn't know where I was, only that my head hurt abominably and my leg was excruciating. The room was dark except for the glow of the quiet, digital machinery. I slowly became aware of wires running all over the place from my body. Monitors. Why did I need monitors? Slowly it came back to me; the tree, falling, branch breaking. I also became aware of something else; I couldn't move. Why? Panic was setting in and I tried to move my arms and legs. I tried to turn and see who else was in the room. No, go. Now panic was really setting in.

I guess my moans and attempts to move alerted whoever was in the room because within a minute a nurse came in and turned on the lights. She came over to check and saw that I was, indeed, awake, well sort of.

"Good to have you back. Just rest quietly. We had to restrain you so you couldn't move around and cause more damage. You have a badly broken leg and a severe concussion. I'll be back in a minute. I need to let the doctor know you're conscious."

I couldn't move so I just blinked my eyes. A shadow fell over my face as someone leaned in front of the lights shining in my eyes. I couldn't see who it was, just sort of a shape of a head.

"Mike, you really had us worried. You'll be okay, son. I'm so glad you're awake. I was so scared." Mom. What was she doing here? I tried to speak but there seemed to be something in my throat. Just then I heard someone come into the room. It was the nurse returning with a doctor.

"Mike. I'm Doctor Mikes. I did the work on your leg. Just relax for a few minutes. We had to restrain you because you were moving around while you were unconscious and we couldn't risk you causing any more damage. Now that you're awake, we'll get those restraints off you." The nurse began unfastening the restraints, starting with the one holding my head. "You can't talk yet, there's a breathing tube in your throat. Do you remember what happened?"

I shook my head 'no'.

"Okay, you broke your leg when it caught in the branch of a tree. That was Saturday afternoon, over three days ago. You also struck your head and have a concussion. I know you're sore. Do you need something for pain?"

I nodded yes, hoping the pain in my head and leg would go away. "Okay, I'll authorize an increase in your medication. You get your rest. I'll check later this morning to see how you're doing." He made a note on my chart and the nurse put something into the IV running into my left arm. Blackness returned.

It was daylight when I regained consciousness. I could tell because the room was brighter even with the lights off. I looked over to my right and saw someone in a chair next to the bed.

"Mike. I'm so glad you're awake. You're goin' to be okay." It was my sister Debra. "We were so scared, so worried. Do you remember what happened? I'll get the nurse. Be right back." I heard her open the door and walk down the hall, returning moments later followed by a different nurse.

"Mike, I'm Michelle, your day nurse. The doctor will be in to remove the tube from your throat in a few minutes. I know you're probably in pain. Do you need anything more? I can increase the dose if the pain is too bad." I shook my head no. She made a few notes on my chart. "I'll just let the doctor know you're awake. Be back in a few minutes." I heard her leave the room.

"Mike, you'll be okay. We'll look after you, all of us. Oh my God, I'm so sorry, so sorry. We shouldn't have let it happen. Gerry is devastated. Says it's his fault." I just shrugged my shoulders. I didn't really know what she was talking about.

"Do you remember climbing the tree?" she asked. I shook my head, no.

"You, Gerry and Jimmy were working in the yard..." she went on to relate the events that led to me lying here in a hospital bed. As she talked parts of what happened were coming back. I clearly remembered the sickening snap as my leg broke.

"...and so you finally woke up three days later. That was around three this morning from what Mom said. We've all been taking turns sitting with you, waiting for you to wake up. We were all so worried, so scared." She was openly weeping by the time she finished.

I was trying to digest all this as the nurse returned, followed shortly after by a doctor. "Mike, I'm going to remove the breathing tube. I don't think you'll need it any more. Your throat will be sore for a couple of days and you probably won't have much of a voice. Don't worry, it's only temporary." He slowly removed the breathing tube from my throat after the nurse turned off the respirator.

"Thank you," I whispered, "head hurts. Leg."

"Yes, you have a severe concussion. Rest will take care of it eventually. It will take some time, but I expect that it will heal completely. Your left leg has a compound fracture just above the ankle. Your leg must have caught in the fork of the tree when you fell. I'm afraid that you're going to be off your feet for quite a while, months anyway."

"Have to get to work," I whispered.

"Not for a while. Your partner will be in later today. He and his wife have come in every day after five to check up on you. He'll fill you in if you're awake." He turned to the nurse and asked about the medication, then made a few notes on the ubiquitous chart. "Okay Mike, I'll check back later. I've left orders to increase the pain medication if needed. You can also have some liquids like soup or broth if you're hungry. We'll wait a couple of days before we try solid food." With a small wave of his hand, he left the room.

The nurse said, "Okay Mike, you're in intensive care, the ICU right now. We'll probably move you out of here tomorrow. If you need anything just push this buzzer. Your family have been with you since the accident, so they'll help as well. Now you behave, I have to check on my other patients." She left the room.

I whispered to Debra, "How long was I out?"

"You were out over three days. We've all been taking turns sitting with you, even Sam and Sonia and Lynsy. Mom and I have been here the most since we don't have jobs. Sam and Sonia have been coming in after the store closes. Oh, that reminds me; I'd better call them and let them know you're awake." She pulled out her cell and called the store. "Sonia, Mike's awake." "Yes, around three this morning and just a few minutes ago." "Yes, of course. We'll see you later."

"She said they'll be in after five. Everyone sends their best. They'll all be in to visit when they can. They just want you to get well. We all do. Now you get your rest or I'll sick the nurse on you."

"Thanks, Sis," I whispered, "tired. Sleep." I drifted off again.

The next day I was moved into a two-bed ward. Over the next few weeks, I slowly healed. My headaches virtually disappeared and I started doing physio to strengthen my leg. I went from wheelchair to crutches relatively quickly, but it would be quite a while until I was in a walking cast. Sam and Sonia ran the business and from what I could gather, it continued to do well. I couldn't wait to get back. All the women, including Lynsy, came and sat with me during the day, taking shifts. Now that I was awake and sort of ambulatory they couldn't see any point in staying overnight.

Gerry was almost a basket case, feeling guilty about the accident until I angrily told him to knock it off. If anything it was my fault for being a dumbass and trying to pretend I was a kid. He stopped blaming himself, at least out loud. We remain friends.

Lynsy came in when she could, and the weekends she had off, she spent most of the day with me. We just relaxed and talked about nothing in particular and visited with all the others who came in. At one point the doctor had to put restrictions on the number of visitors since everyone wanted to come in, and it seemed all at once. When it became evident that one of my family or Lynsy would spend days with me, they allowed only two other visitors at a time.

Lynsy and I were becoming more and more comfortable with each other. My Mom and Lynsy's parents were happy, even relieved, to see us together after everything that had happened. My Mom told me that it was Lynsy who sat with me all Saturday night after I came out of the OR, and most of Sunday until they almost physically kicked her out of the hospital to go home and get some rest. She did have to work the next day, after all.

About six weeks after being admitted to hospital I was discharged. Since I still needed care, I would be staying with my Mom in her apartment. It was two bedrooms on the ground floor of a +55 complex. She had received special permission for me to stay as long as necessary. As tiring as it was, I was happy to be out of the hospital and able to at least go outside and sit in the late autumn sun.

The store had reopened a day later than planned because of my accident. It looked like turning the whole thing into an internet cafe might work. We were still busy with repairs and network maintenance. The only difference, other than me not being there, was that Sonia was doing the paperwork that was usually my burden. I even missed that, since it gave me a real sense of how we were doing. They were still looking for someone to help Mary. She was just as busy now as she had been when the restaurant was a separate entity. That was something we would really have to work at.

Jimmy came over to Mom's to visit one afternoon. He and Jane were still a couple and he was planning on popping the big question soon. Jane wasn't working but did some volunteer work at the seniors' centre in town. There wasn't really much work available for her in town. I asked him what she was actually trained to do. It turns out that she had a college certificate in business administration. I asked Jimmy to get her to come over and see me. I gave Mary a call.

"Mary, hi. How are you?"

"Mike. Hi. We're busy. I think I'm busier now than ever. We really do need some help here." Mary sounded almost rushed. "I heard. Sorry I haven't been around to help. But, I just wanted your input. I might have someone who would fit in. Do you want to interview her, or be here when I talk to her?"

"Well, I sort of trust your judgement, but I'd like input as well."

"Of course. Look, I'm waiting for her to call me. If I set something up for an evening, would you be available?"

"Sure, anytime after supper would work."

"Okay, as soon as I get this set up I'll call you. I don't even know if the person I'm thinking of is interested, but she might be since she's not working, at least not being paid, anyway."

"Okay Mike, let me know. I gotta run." She ended the call and I sat back thinking that it was good to be back at it, even if in a limited way. I had a doctors' appointment the next day. I was really hoping to be cleared to go back to work. I could at least do the admin stuff and free up Sonia from that. Mom came out of the apartment and sat down at the picnic table. "Mike, have you had your nap yet this afternoon?"

"Nope, I really don't feel tired."

"You know what Dr Mikes said. You need rest, lots of rest. I'll report you," she laughed as if threatening me would get me to co-operate. "Okay, okay. I'll go lie down. But, if Jane calls I need to talk to her. I might have a job if she's interested." I wheeled myself into the spare bedroom that had become my home. "Okay, but you rest or even worse than reporting you to the doctor, I'll report you to your sisters," she was laughing out loud now.

"Oh God, anything but that. I'll behave. Honest." I managed to get onto the bed unaided and was quickly asleep. I must have slept for nearly two hours. Jane had phoned and would call back or I could call her when I woke up. Mom got some coffees going and we went back outside to enjoy the sunshine. I called Jane on her cell.

"Hi Jane, Mike. Look. Are you looking for work at all or just want to do the volunteer stuff?"

"Mike, Jimmy told me to call you. What's this about, anyway?"

"If you're interested, I might have a job for you. Jimmy said you had your two-year certification in business administration. If you're looking for work, this might be a good fit for you."

"You mean I'd be working for you?"

"No, not for me. For a friend of mine. She's looking for help."

"Where do I have to go to meet her?"

"Actually, she said she'd come here almost any time after supper so it sort of depends on you."

"How about tonight? I'll get Jimmy to bring me over."

"Okay, I'll call Mary and get back to you. If not tonight is any other night okay with you?"

"Oh sure, we don't do much at night. Just hang out and watch TV."

"Okay, I'll call you back."

"Thanks, Mike. Talk to you soon."

I broke the connection an began to call Mary when Mom said, "Mike, why not ask Mary to come here for supper. She and I can visit until Jane gets here. I'm sure she could use the break. I know it's a bit of a drive, but if she's coming over anyway..."

"Good idea, Mom. Thanks." I called Mary who said she'd be delighted to eat someone else's cooking for a change. I called Jane who confirmed that she and Jimmy would show up after supper. Mom said for them to come over too, she would make enough for all of us. They of course agreed. There's nothing like Mom's cooking.

Mary arrived just before six, bringing a nice bottle of wine. She and Mom had met several times and got along great. Jimmy and Jane showed up a few minutes later and we all sat down to dinner, breaded pork chops, mashed potatoes and mixed veggies. The four of them enjoyed the wine; I wasn't allowed because of the painkillers I was still on.

Instead of doing a formal interview, we just asked Jane about her background and what she was looking for. She admitted that she had no experience in the food industry at all, not even working as a server when she was in school. We explained to her that she would start out working alongside Mary who would teach her that aspect of the internet cafe, with a view that Mary would eventually retire and sell the business and building, hopefully to me. Jane was sceptical, but agreed to give it a trial run.

The worst that could happen is that she'd have another line on her resume'. We agreed that she would start the following Monday, giving her a few days to prepare. We had to assure her that casual dress was appropriate. Anything more would really look out of place. Even Sonia had stopped wearing dresses or skirts to work, settling on Capris or slacks; shorts if it was really hot outside. We retired to the living room and enjoyed visiting over coffee and dessert for the rest of the evening.

Next afternoon was time to see the doctor about getting back to work. Except for my leg, which both ached and itched like crazy, I felt good. I expected that he would approve it, and he did. I decided that I would start back the following Monday since there was only one more work day before the weekend. We had kept Mary's tradition of closing for the entire weekend. I was looking forward to it, though I would have to rely on Mom to get me to work. I'd get Sam or Sonia to bring me back. Once I had a walking cast on, I would return to my apartment. Debra had assured Mom that she would look in on me to make sure everything was okay.

Monday I got to the store early. The interior was bright and cheery. Knocking out the one wall between the two businesses had really opened it up and gave an impression of being larger than it really was. We had gotten some additional space for the workshop by combining the storage area of the two stores, except for the cold foods. It wasn't unusual to see bags of flour sitting alongside network cables or computer parts. Soon it was just the way it was.

Jane started and fitted right in. Her personality more than made up for her lack of experience and she proved to be a quick study. We arranged, and paid, for her to take her food safety course. We were able to keep the two entities separate and never did have to call on anyone in the computer store to work in the cafe or vice versa. Even though I was more or less stuck behind my desk, it felt really good to be back. I called my customers and apologized for not being able to look after them myself. To a man or woman, they were all understanding and looked forward to seeing me again when I was able.

Lynsy and I managed to get together a couple of times a week, even if just for coffee. Of course, she had to come to me since I couldn't drive yet because of the concussion.

Some evenings we'd just relax in front of the tube. We were getting along just fine and we're feeling good about it. I wondered about moving to the next level, but wanted to wait until I at least had a walking cast on and I was more mobile. She was feeling the same, but had other plans about the timing.

One evening we were in our normal positions me stretched out on the sofa to keep my leg elevated and her relaxing in the recliner. She had just gone to get some iced tea for both of us. When she came back into the living room, instead of sitting back in the recliner, she came over and sat me up an sat down on the sofa, then pulled me back down so my head and shoulders were on her lap.

She leaned down and gave me a kiss, then another one, longer this time. "Mike, you know I love you."

"Mmmm. I love you too, you know. I know it's kind of quick, but it feels right, the two of us together," I sighed happily. "I'll be so happy to get the damn cast off and get my life back." She began to rub my chest, then lower and lower. "I think we could take this to the bedroom." She leaned down and kissed me again. "You just let me do all the hard work."

I laughed, "I was hoping to take a more active part."

"Just do what you can. I'll look after us," she said quietly, pushing me up off her lap and helping me to my feet. I still had to use the crutches so the walk into the bedroom wasn't all that romantic. We made it.

We made love for what seemed hours. It wasn't of course since I didn't have the stamina. It felt so good to have her back in my arms, and I told her so. "I've wanted this for so long," she said quietly, "I wondered if the day would ever come when I'd feel happy again."

"I know what you mean. It's almost like I was going through the motions."

"Exactly." She stopped me from talking further by kissing me again. "Now, lover, I have to get going. I have to work early in the morning. I'll take a quick shower here so I don't have to in the morning."

"I'd join you, but it's hard enough for me by myself, let alone with someone else," I laughed. "Now get going while I still have a bit of willpower left." She giggled and climbed out of the bed. Soon the shower was running. It did feel right.

Epilogue

Lynsy and I waited for nearly nine months to get married. We honeymooned in Hawaii for two glorious weeks. She continued working at the lab until our son was born a year after we got married. He was joined by twins, a boy and a girl, about eight-teen months later. She's now quite happy to be a homemaker and mother.

The business continued to expand. We eventually had to move the computer store to its own building. The internet cafe doubled in size, and they added a small retail bakery and goodies store.

Jane and Jimmy got married. He's now the manager of the auto parts store. Jane manages the internet cafe and has four girls working full time for her. Lynsy and I are considering making her and Jimmy partners as well.

Mary did what she wanted to do, she sold the building to me and retired to the coast to be near her family. She keeps in touch with us and visits when she can.

Sam and Sonia added to their brood, two boys. The girls were thrilled to have one baby brother; the second sent them over the moon. Sonia is a stay at home mom now. They bought the house across the street from us. Our two families are always together.

Debra and Gerry continue to do well. They haven't been able to have kids, but have adopted ours, and Sam and Sonia's, as their extended family. Of course, they spoil the kids rotten.

Mom passed away a few months after our son was born. She was really happy to see her first grandchild though she was in poor health at the time. It was sad to see her go. She was a great Mom.

Lori and Mandy also got married. They had to have a civil ceremony. Of course, all of us were there as well as all their friends and customers. They're talking about adopting a couple of kids to make a whole family unit.

I look back at all that happened, everything we went through, and thank my lucky stars that That Was Then, This is Now.

THE END

Printed in Poland
by Amazon Fulfillment
Poland Sp. z o.o., Wrocław